you have
a piece of my

heart

YOU HAVE A PIECE OF MY HEART

A COLLECTION OF SHORT STORIES

WILLOW WINTERS

Copyright © 2021 by Willow Winters

All rights reserved.

No part of this book may be reproduced in any form or by any electronic or mechanical means, including information storage and retrieval systems, without written permission from the author, except for the use of brief quotations in a book review.

Cover Design by Lori Jackson Design

TOO MUCH WORK & NOT ENOUGH PLAY

CHARLIE

Keys, wallet: check and check. My mental list doesn't stop there as I glance at the clock in my office of the bar. I'm going to be late. *Fuck*. Grace is going to kill me.

Flipping through each of the order sheets, listening to the tick of the clock and trying to focus on this stack of papers and not the others, all I can think about is the last time I was late.

I missed our son's entire appointment. My gaze involuntarily darts to a photo of our little man in a simple black frame on my desk. Besides a pen that states: World's Best Dad, the picture is the only thing personal in this room. That and the framed photo of Grace and I on our wedding day. It's almost been a year and time has flown by. The days seem shorter and the years faster. I don't know how to slow it all down.

I've already missed more than I ever thought I would.

With the faint smell of beer and the clink of bottles being carted through the bar on the other side of the closed door of my office in Mac's bar – my bar – I remember how Grace smiled and said it was okay. It's not a real smile though, not one that reached her eyes.

So when she tells me over and over again that she can't keep doing it all herself, I know she can't. I know things have to change.

Knock, knock, knock. The thud resonates in my office and I clear my throat before telling Maggie she can come in.

With both fists on her hips, she stands in the doorway, her hair swept into a wild bun on top of her head.

"Yeah?" I question, noting that her apron must've just come out of the dryer. Either that or its brand new. *Eric did say we needed new ones; did he order them?*

"What the hell are you doing here?" Maggie's head tilts with her question and her dark eyes narrow. "Your mother will have a fit."

My wife will too. I keep my comment to myself,

my lips thinning into a straight line as Mags crosses her arms.

Behind her the chatter from the bar is barely heard, but the clanking from the kitchen and a laugh from James lets me know the bar is in full swing.

"Are you sure you've got this--"

"All taken care of?" she finishes my question for me and then tells me to get lost and go have some fun.

"Alright then. I was just leaving." Letting the stack of papers fall back onto my desk with a dull thud, I check my back pocket again and then grab my keys.

"Tell Cheryl I said hi," Mags tells me and then turns, but quickly turns back, her hand on the door jam and asks in a hushed voice, "Is she pregnant again?"

Ooh how this small town loves to whisper.

"Have a good night Mags," I answer her, well not so much answer as shut her down, with a grin and scoot past her.

The new equipment in the kitchen makes the old oven look even older. It's the only thing back here that hasn't been updated. I make a mental note to ask Eric about that too.

Too many changes, too many moving parts to keep up with now that the bar has expanded. A sigh leaves me and the keys in my hand jingle.

Time to see my wife, the thought brings a smile to lift my lips up until I see the time.

Shit.

I love Grace so damn much and I want to be the husband she deserves and the father my son needs.

"*I* cannot believe it's been a year," Ali leans back in the plastic lawn chair, the front legs slipping up in the thick green grass of Cheryl's backyard. "It's crazy," she murmurs.

"It's been one wonderful year though," Cheryl replies, lifting the water bottle in a mock cheers to Ali, who in turn lifts her pink vodka lemonade cocktail up and the two women wait for me.

"Cheers to that," I join in, balancing the punch I have in my left hand with the bouncing baby in my lap steadied with my right. Little Dean. "Happy Anniversary Ali," I add sincerely.

"Almost a year for you too!" Her smile broadens and she taps the paper cup on the table before lifting it back up for another drink.

I opted for the punch, thinking it wouldn't be as

strong as what Ali's drinking. She was already a little tipsy when we got here at a quarter to 6. It was my mistake though. Joseph must've poured an entire bottle of rum into that bowl.

Another sip and my eyes squint. I'm going to have to be careful when I pour this red concoction into the grass and then I'll have what Ali's having.

"Yes, all the summer anniversaries," Cheryl squeals, holding her belly and searching across the yard for her little girl Evie, who's squealing joyfully and chasing bubbles from a bubble machine. My mother-in-law, Cheryl and Ali's mother, is watching Evie. She offered to watch Dean too and snuggle with him, but he needs to nap first. Resting his head on my shoulder, the sigh is audible and he goes into his routine of that little hand holding on to my thumb as he nestles down.

"Velcro baby," Cheryl whispers and it makes me smile. Ma, as my mother-in-law told me to call her, gets my little man during the day every day practically, so this nap is mine. All the snuggles.

"Yeah it's all going according to plan," a familiar voice speaks over my shoulder. I glance, along with Ali and Cheryl to see both Eric, the manager at my husband's bar, tall and lean with dirty blonde hair and soft wrinkles around his eyes from too much time under the Atlanta sun and next to him, my husband.

As handsome and charming as ever. His broad

shoulders show themselves off in his simple white tee, stretching the thin fabric that puts his biceps on display. Almost a year of marriage and a sleepless 3-month old hasn't changed the spark between us. Maybe the honeymoon phase is waning but I think that's because both of us work far too much which leaves little time for just the two of us. They're going over business more than likely. With a deep breath in, I continue rocking Dean, who's nodding off to sleep, completely unaware that his father is just behind him. If he knew, he'd shoot right back up and fight off sleep just to look at his Daddy. He loves his father, he should after all, he looks just like him.

"Do you even want to know what time it is?" Ali asks under her breath practically shooting lasers out of her eyes at Charlie.

"We knew he'd be late," I comment half-heartedly. I can pretend it doesn't get to me, but he's missing so much of Dean's life. His first appointments, his first smile, which happened when I showed little Dean the picture of Charlie hanging from his mobile before trying to get him to sleep in his crib.

"We're both tired, just trying to balance it all," I give the excuse to Ali although I can't look her in the eye and opt for another swig of that punch.

We've been working so hard we barely had a Christmas, a New Year… any holiday at all. I suppose that's what happens when two workaholics get together.

"Almost a year since my shotgun wedding and I don't think he's shown up on time to a single thing since then."

That gets a laugh from the gaggle of women around the table under the white tent. The fresh scent from the gorgeous bouquet of hydrangeas engulfs me as a decent breeze blows by. It's a little on the too-warm side for a July evening, but the company makes it all worth it. The spiked punch and the shade from the tent don't hurt either. Even if the rum is already hitting me.

"Shotgun schmotgun," Aliana comments. "You were swept away in a… what do they call it?"

"A whirlwind romance," Cheryl answers with her hand splayed over her heart and a faraway look on her face. *She's such a romantic.*

I don't want to admit it, but sitting here now, thinking about that honeymoon phase, maybe some of that spark has faded. Too busy to… well to get busy. It used to be that he couldn't keep his hands off of me. I still want him though. I still love him… even more now than before.

"And this little one is already such a big boy," Cheryl gratefully changes the subject and my mind focuses on what she said rather than what I was thinking.

"You have lost your mind. Dean is only 3 months old. Keep my baby a baby, Aunt Cheryl."

"Time is flying isn't it?" The women reminisce and my worries come right back.

CHARLIE

Over the span of 20 minutes and after only sneaking a peck on the cheek to both my son and wife, both of my brother-in-laws have come to the same conclusion.

I need to fuck my wife.

No shit. The bastards think it's funny. She saw me but didn't make a move. Didn't say hi, barely even gave me a smile. My nerves pricked when I made my way to her after Eric finally let me go. I snuck in a kiss on her cheek and one on a sleeping Dean and since then, all I've done is take crap from these two.

"What's keeping you from having baby number 2?" my brother-in-law nudges my ribs and the other lets out a chuckle before calling 'hey now' at my little niece who takes a tumble while being chased by my pa. His words register, but I focus my attention on Grace.

"Burgers almost done?" Joseph questions Michael and the spices from sausages and grilled meat join the breeze as the men open the grill.

I can't hear what Grace is telling Ma as she rocks in place, tapping a sleeping Dean's bottom. I'm certain she's asking if my mother wants to cuddle with Dean or if Grace should tuck him in inside. There's a playpen just inside and the baby monitor is already hooked up with the other piece of it sitting on the outdoor foldout table the ladies are all gathered around.

Grace is utterly breath-taking in that yellow dress. I heard someone one night say yellow is a happy color, it makes you happy to just look at it.

I don't know if it's true, but the butterflies in my chest are more than pleased when I take her in. Another part of my anatomy is also more than pleased. When Grace turns with a smile, her dress swaying as she heads to the backdoor with our son in her arms, I toss the empty bottle of beer and ignore my brother-in-laws as I follow Grace inside.

The screen door creaks and I stop it from shutting so I can come in. That's the moment Grace notices me and she shushes me, still cradling our son.

As if I didn't know he was napping. Giving her a nod, she keeps moving, a simper gracing her gorgeous face and those doe eyes softening just for me.

If she was mad that I was late, she doesn't appear to be now.

"We'll just let him sleep for an hour," she whispers after gently laying Dean down in the playpen.

"Sounds good to me," I keep my voice low and my eyes go wide for just a moment when Dean stirs. My heart freezes and my lungs hold steady until Dean coos in his sleep and snuggles down.

"Oh thank goodness," Grace's shoulders shake with a small laugh and her hand splayed across her chest and a wide smile on her lips.

She tries to leave the way she came, but my arm wraps around her waist.

"Not yet," I whisper in the crook of her neck and plant a kiss there. Her gasp is audible and I can't help but to glance at Dean.

"What are you--?" she tries to question and I pull her along behind me. There's a guest room in this house.

As I tug her hand and we stop in the hallway, Grace smacks my hand away. "What are you thinking Charlie?"

I'm thinking desperate times call for desperate measures, but I don't tell her that.

My hand finds the dip in her waist and I look my

wife in her eyes to tell her, "I miss you. I need you. And I want you right fucking now."

"Charlie," she gasps again and the tension between us sparks. Every inch of me hotter and needing to be inside her, making her moan, watching her eyes go half lidded. I need that. She needs it too.

"Remember at the wedding, my sister's wedding?" I question her, my memory taking me back to a certain coat closet where everything about us changed for me. My heart locked in on her and right now having her and making sure she knows I love her and I want her just the same now as I did then is more important than going out in the backyard to chat with family we still see every Sunday night.

"Charlie," Grace admonishes me, but her lips stay parted and lust coats my name on her lips.

"Yeah sweetheart," I question, taking a half step closer to her, and letting my hands fall to her ass. "Are you going to make me beg? Cause I'd rather hear you begging me for more if we've only got a few minutes."

The blush I knew was coming lights up her cheeks, nearly turning them the shade of red of her gorgeous locks.

"Come on, I urge her, looking past her towards the back door of the house to see no one's there and opening the door to the guest room.

It's not dark at all with the bright light shining

through the white curtains. But there's privacy. No one to see us, no one to hear us, the window is closed shut. Seeing the bed made perfectly, I decide in a split second, I'm fucking her against the wall.

"I think-" Grace starts and I close the door behind her, locking it and pressing my lips to hers before she can say another word. She's shocked at first, but her lips mold to mine quickly and she moans into my mouth as her seam parts, granting me entry and her hands find my hair, spearing through it.

Gracing my fingers along the smooth skin of her legs, I let them drift up her dress and find her underwear. When I slip them down, I have to break the kiss and Grace takes that moment to let her head fall back against the wall I'm about to fuck her against.

"We really shouldn't," she breathes the statement with her eyes closed, her skin already flushed and her nails digging into my shoulders.

"You want me?" I question her, already unbuttoning my pants and then the sound of the zipper dropping fills the silence and brings her deep gaze to mine.

"Always," she answers in a whisper and I'm quick to grab her ass with both hands, listening to that sweet gasp of surprise that's only muted by another heated kiss.

It takes a moment to bring her dress up around her hips and position her how I want her.

Grace's heels dig into my ass as my jeans fall to the floor. "It'll be quick," I tell Grace in between nibbles of her bottom lip. Her chest rises and falls with quickened breaths and she nods and then steals a kiss I intended for her throat. She knows what she wants. My sweetheart always has. I should have listened to this woman sooner. So many different times and for so many different reasons.

Fisting my cock, I press the head against her lips, parting them and slowly pushing myself inside of her. The sweet strangled moan from Grace that mixes with our warm breath fuels me to go slower, to make love to her for as long as I can before fucking her raw and hard like I so desperately want to.

I take my time, feeling her tight and hot around me. "Always so fucking wet," I groan in the crook of her neck, loving the pleasure she gives me and loving how she makes those little moans of sweet satisfaction as I rock myself inside of her.

Her teeth graze along my neck when I kiss her just under her ear, right at the sensitive spot she loves so much. It sends goosebumps along her skin and the way she writhes as I pull out and then push myself deeper inside of her, begs my body to thrust harder and faster, but I take my time.

"Charlie," she mewls and that right there is why I don't rush it. I love it when she begs for more. More of me, more of us.

"Yeah sweetheart," I pull out of her nearly all the way and bracing her against the wall with one arm, I move the pad of my thumb to her clit before she can answer.

Capturing her gasp with my lips, I spread her arousal around her swollen nub and piston my hips just a bit faster.

Her body tightens around me, her breath hitches and those heels dig harder into my ass. It takes everything in me not to rut into her faster, but the wait is worth it. It's always worth it with her.

Her silent scream is complete with her hand slapping against the wall, a strangled yes leaving her lips and her release feeling like heaven on my cock.

"My turn," I warn, the words slipping against her lips as her eyes find mine and I fuck her against the wall like we don't have a second to waste.

I take my wife like I did that night in the coat room of the wedding. I fuck her like I'm going to lose her if I don't make damn sure she knows she's mine.

She is today, she was back then, and she always will be.

When I find my own release, she comes again with me, and we're lost in a heated kiss that's not at all lust and all love. Every little piece of us finding its place where it's supposed to be.

GRACE

*H*ow long has it been since I've held my husband's hand? I wonder as we quietly leave our still napping baby boy, and gently shut the screen door so we don't wake him.

Charlie's thumb rubs soothing circles on my knuckles, the rough pads remind me how hard he works, but also how hard he loves.

"Love you sweetheart," he whispers as the bright sun and chatter of the barbeque greet us and we part ways with a simple kiss that makes its way all the way down to my toes. I can still feel him and I love it. The second he's gone though, back to where the men are grilling, stacks of burgers on a plate surrounded by condiments on the small table beside them, I wonder if it's written on my face what we've done.

With a quick breath, I don't look anyone in the

eyes and I go straight for the punch. One sip and I can hear the laughter from Evie. Another and I make my way back to my seat with my sister in laws.

"Did he wake up?" Cheryl questions, the girls, now joined by Charlie's mother, all stop talking and wait for an answer, their eyes expecting something right freaking now.

"Yeah," I play it off even though my head shakes, subconsciously denying the lie. "The second I laid him down, he woke up, but we were able to get him back down in no time."

Even though I catch a glimpse of the monitor on the table and Ali's raised brow, I double down with, "He's out like a light," and my third sip of punch. It's not so strong now and I wonder if someone added more of anything other than rum to dull it down.

None of the women push for more, but my two sister-in-laws both smile into their drinks as Ma continues, informing me that she's giving the girls the recipe to her pasta salad.

"Well hello beautiful," Charlie sneaks up behind me, his hands landing on my hips and a kiss landing on my cheek before I even see him.

I can't help but smile. "Hello yourself," I answer with a little more flirtation than I would if I was more conscious of the fact that all three women are staring. "You might need this if you were drinking the punch," he passes me a bottle of water and I let out a shy laugh.

"You might be right."

"I have one little surprise if you ladies," he raises his voice to address his family, "don't mind if I steal her away."

"You just had her but okay," Cheryl rolls her eyes and I try to keep mine from widening at *you just had her*. They don't know, I tell myself with every step I take to the side of the property with Charlie, where the sunflowers are tall and blooming.

"Okay, now that I have you sweetened up," he starts, and I smack his hand playfully. His rough chuckle vibrates up his chest and I land a quick kiss on his lips.

"What do you want, husband of mine?"

He sucks in a deep breath, his expression going serious and for a moment worry comes over me. Until he says:

"We didn't have a Christmas so I decided a little July surprise… would be nice."

"Oh yeah, it's Christmas in July?" I question him, my brow knitting.

What's my husband up to?

"I thought Ali could come with us since she's got time off… and kind of volunteered… maybe on a trip to wine country? She can watch Dean and we can have a second honeymoon."

I can only blink several times, my heart going all soft.

"You won't be away from Dean… although he will be in a different room," he explains, the water bottle in his hand moving from his left to his right as he shifts on his feet in front of me. "I miss you all alone, flirting at the bar. I just thought…"

"What are you thinking?" I press him for more, reaching out with both hands to hold on to his shirt and looking my husband in the eyes.

"We have at least another 18 or more years of mom and dad life, and I love it. I really do, but I want some nights where it's just the two of us, so I can tease you. Eric is hiring another manager. I'm stepping back. I'm going to be the owner, instead of a worker. I'm stepping back like you wanted sweetheart. I promise I am."

"Can you do that?" I'm breathless with anticipation and shock.

"We can afford it," he answers with a single nod.

"I mean *can you* do that," stressing the question.

My husband takes a half step forward, folding his arms around me and pulling me in so he's only a handful of inches away from me. "What I can't do is continue to come home after my son is already in bed. I can't keep missing you either. Missing us and the memories we should be making." He adds, "Your weekends are with the family and now mine are too."

"You promise?" I can't believe he's actually doing it. I'm so happy I could cry. I know it may take time though. The bar was his baby before I came along and stole him away.

He states proudly, "I'm also declaring Fridays date nights and between your mom and sister, Maggie, and my sisters and mom, we have plenty of sitters…"

I stop him here, kissing him like a mad woman, my arms flying around his neck. When I break the kiss, I tell him I love him.

He doesn't have to tell me he loves me too; I know he does, but he says the words just the same.

We had a whirlwind romance and all I want to do is hold on to it forever.

If you haven't read **Knocking Boots**, Charlie and Grace's standalone sexy, contemporary romance, click **here** to read today and get caught up in their sweet love story.

STAY RIGHT HERE WITH ME

I can't tell you how many mistakes I've made sitting in this very spot in this small town bar. Watching the iron doors swing closed as the broad-shouldered man who just walked in sits across from me, I already know he's on that list of, "I shouldn't have done that..."

LYSA

"Make it shine," my grandma used to tell me that whenever I was cleaning the bar top. I had a habit of it when I was only four years old. She told me all about it when I got my first job here, the bar called Brick's that used to belong to my grandfather. I thought she was lying at first when she told me, but the customers remembered it too. I'd take the little cloth rag from the little tykes kitchen in the backroom and I'd climb up the wooden barstools and get on top of the already polished bar top and mimic my father. Three small circles, then one large. My little arms couldn't reach all the way across, but I kept going when Grandma told me, "Make it shine."

With the fresh smell of pine and lemons lingering, I make three small circles against the hardwood top, worn down from years of doing its job, and whisper, "Make it shine," with the last swirl.

I've spent long days and even longer nights in this bar. It used to only be the weekends but now it's every day for almost three years now when the bar got passed to me. It should never have been mine at the young age of twenty-two, but life throws all sorts of things at you, and you just have to do your best to catch them. Yet another piece of advice from my grandma.

"You good wrapping this up?" Andy asks me on his way out. With his worn leather jacket in one hand, its creases matching the ones around his eyes, and his car keys in the other, the old man waits for me to tell him what I always tell him at 2 am.

"Darn right I am. Have a good night, Andy." His gray beard leads the way as he gives me a smile. I've nearly turned away when I hear a sound of surprise come from him.

"You may have company," he informs me with a raised brow and I'm already saying, "We're closed," from across the bar to the heavy front doors but then I get a peek of who it is on the other side.

Flip, twist, a little somersault happens inside my chest. His blue eyes meet mine first, even though he's nodding a thanks to Andy as he takes his baseball cap off. His stature is dominating, as are his broad shoulders, when the man walks in, his boot steps taking their time and thumping right along with my heart.

Tall, dark and handsome, with a slight southern charm on his tanned skin. Jeans that look broken into, boots made for working, and a simple dark gray Henley stretched across his shoulders fit his frame and spell out my kryptonite. The man of my dreams is a real thing.

"It's alright Andy… I think I can serve up one more drink." Pulling out a bottle of beer from the fridge underneath the bar, I keep my eyes on the man who just walked in. In a deft motion I uncap it, the piece of tin falling into the bucket beneath the bottle opener screwed into the bar top and place the glass bottle down onto the bar, listening to it fizz. "As in I can open a bottle of beer. I'm not washing any more glasses tonight."

I've made a number of mistakes in my life and one time my father said they could all lead back to my attitude. He laughed when I reminded him that it's his attitude I inherited so technically they could all lead back to him.

Maybe I am no-nonsense, but when you grow up in a bar you learn not to take any shit and to know your limits. I'll be damned if I'm cleaning anything else tonight. Besides, the man of my dreams is an IPA kind of man.

"Thanks," his voice is deep and has a draw to it

that I love. It echoes down into the hollow of my chest and I find myself raising my hand to meet the vibrations.

"Have a long night?" I make small talk with him as I tidy up the place. Technically we're closed, technically I'm not working anymore, technically Mr. Tall, Dark and Handsome shouldn't be here.

In my periphery, I watch him fiddle with the torn edge of his hat before tossing it down onto the bar and taking his seat. "Long week," he finally tells me with a heavy sigh. "Just got a lot better though."

I pay his compliment back with a small chuckle that warms me from the inside and ask back, "Oh, did it now? A beer can turn it all around for you."

I stare at him, letting his gaze sink into mine and feeling the longing and the heat there.

He only offers a boyish grin, answering, "Something like that," with the bottle neck of his beer at his lips before taking a long swig.

"How about you?"

"How about me what?" I ask him, blowing a stray stand of hair out of my face. I note that his is long on top, just long enough to make it look like he doesn't care. Like he's just rough around the edges. *I like that.*

"Long night?" he asks.

"Always," I answer, finally taking a seat behind the counter. My back hurts, my body's sore, but we did good this week. I put everything I have into this bar. Keeping it alive and just like it was in every way that I can remember. It's my constant, my life really. Everyone I ever loved has memories in this bar. So it can have all of me. I'm fine with that.

"You ready to go home? I don't want to keep you up."

Home for me is just a walk next door. My dogs outside stay in the back behind the bar and the German Shepherds walk me down the stone path to my little raised ranch. They're my babies and the only family I have left.

The second that house next to the bar went up for sale, I bought it. I was only twenty and my dad had to help me, but it's mine and it's the perfect set up. I have my dogs, the bar, I have my house, and I have the people who have been here all my life in this small town. And then there's this man right here.

I try to ease his conscious, "You aren't keeping me up."

"You look tired."

"Hmmm," I hum and lean back so I can get a good look at him.

"I don't mind walking you home and helping you get to sleep," he offers with that smile I love.

"Dean Andrews, you are the biggest mistake I ever made." I love saying his name. Dean Andrews. Grandma loved it too. She always shooed the guys away, but never Dean. I could curse her out for that with the way he's played with my heart. But then she'd slap me silly and I was always taught to respect my elders anyhow.

"Made as in past tense?" he offers me a charming asymmetric smile. "I was hoping you weren't done with me yet." That smile is one that knows how to bring heat to my cheeks, a blush rising up my temples. No man has ever made me feel like he does. Maybe that's why I just can't say no.

I don't answer him, wiping down the rest of the liquor bottles, even though I've already wiped them down once, with my back to him. Very well aware that my hips sway just slightly with every movement I make. Let him watch. Let him want me even though he's not able to have me. It's only fair.

"You come into town once a month for a weekend, maybe twice a month at most… and you think you aren't a mistake for a girl like me?" I question him, peeking over my shoulder just in time to see him gaze shift from my ass up to my stern gaze. He knows I'm all his. He knows I'll bring him home and my bed will be filled with both of us tonight. This push and pull is just a game.

A game that's going to break my heart one day. Since I gave it to Dean Andrews and he doesn't even know. Shoot, I didn't even know I'd done it until it was too late.

DEAN

It's been at least four years since I first saw Lysa Hart. My father was showing me *"a hole in the wall"* bar he'd found. Since I was a little kid, every summer I'd gone with him in his truck for the rides during the summer. My dad's a truck driver, my uncle, my brother. So it just made sense to me that I would be too.

I was twenty-three and I'd had my own truck for a while when my dad brought me in here four years ago. Craft beers, football games, a pool table and a small town vibe that made you feel at home. That's what he told me it was like, but when I walked through those doors, there was only one thing that felt like home to me.

It was her laugh that I heard first, and I caught her swinging her hair around to the other shoulder and telling someone to 'shut their mouth' before swatting them with an imaginary towel. Her long hair matched her deep brown eyes and her smile… her smile was everything.

It only took one look… and that was years ago. Just before her life changed forever.

I work on drinking the beer quickly, knowing she's got to want to get out of here.

"How long have you been on the road?" she asks; she only ever makes small talk. The thing I learned about Lysa first was how guarded she was. She could make friends with anyone, but to get to know her took time. And I know her, I know every little thing about her. Because after I'm inside her, after pulling down all of those walls and giving her everything I have, she bares it all. Heart and soul.

"Came in from Georgia, so a little while I guess," I joke and she winces, the idea of spending nearly ten hours on the road isn't her kind of fun. I don't mind it. With the audio books and the sites along the way, it's been good to me. But she's better.

Every time I come back, Lysa's made at least one change to the bar, this time the felt on the pool table's new. She does that, trying to keep the place updated… but a few things never change.

"Still have the photos up?" I question although the answer is clear. The photograph paper is yellowed from decades and decades of simply existing. Lysa's done a hell of a lot to fix up the old bar, but she's stuck in the past in a lot of ways. Understandably. "You could move them to the backroom you know?" I suggest for the second time. The first was a year ago, maybe more. I know she wants to move them because they just look dated, but she's dead set on the fact that they belong there.

A brunette lock slips out of place from her bun of messy hair, falling gently against the curve of Lysa's jaw when she turns to look over her shoulder.

I know her body better than I know the backroads. And damn do I miss it every time I leave. I spent my life in a truck, she spent hers in this bar. Both of us taking after our fathers.

"I just don't want to move them; you know?"

"I get it, it just might help bring the bar up to this decade… or," I offer up, "You could take it back. You know, make it look like a speakeasy or something? Isn't that the look that your grandpa went for back then?"

I've been thinking a lot about this bar and what Lysa could do on little money and even short time.

She laughs at me, "No. It was not a speakeasy. It was a biker club." The hint of a smile at her lips is addictive.

"Make it a biker club then," I shrug knowing damn well what she's going to say.

"In a small town with no bikers, I bet that would go over just wonderfully."

"You know what they say, you build it and they'll come."

She shrugs it off, tiredness forces a yawn out of her.

I finish off the last bit of my beer and the empty bottle clinks when I set it back down.

"You want to get out of here?" she asks me.

No. I don't want to get out of here. I want to stay with her and bring that smile, sweet and innocent, full of hope, back to her beautiful face. Just like it was when I first saw her. I want to stay here and fix this with her. Sometimes though… all a person can do is stand beside them and wait.

"If you do," I answer her, lowering my voice and letting my gaze drop to those lips of hers. Lips I dream about kissing every night. She parts them just slightly, taking in a sharp inhale. "Yeah," I tell her, pushing myself off the stool and grabbing my cap. "Let's get out of here."

*I*t's quiet between us all the way to my house, the dogs padding along as Dean pats them and occasionally scratches their backs on the way.

The crickets are out, the early autumn night has just a slight chill to it, but still warm enough. And the moon is clear, shining down and giving me enough light to see the rough stubble on Dean's jaw.

He keeps his arm around my waist the entire walk and it makes me feel weak because all I want to do is lean into him.

The backdoor shuts with a loud groan and I lock it, feeling Dean's eyes on me. The house has charm and features from a century ago. Just like the bar. It's expensive to maintain, but every penny tile, and carved molding feature is worth it.

Some people say I'm an old soul. I just think I have good taste.

Dean doesn't waste his time taking off his boots and stretching out his back. Maybe he's trying to hide it, but I know he's tired too.

"You want to just go to bed?" I ask him, feeling a ping of vulnerability. He could stay at the truck stop, and sleep in the back of his truck like I know he used to. He could get a hotel. Or he can come here, where I give everything to him freely. My girlfriend Laura had something to say about that a while back. Two years ago before she moved to Texas with her boyfriend, now husband.

I told her then, I do what feels right. And Dean… everything about him feels right. Up until he's gone, that is.

"I want you in bed, if that's what you mean." His strong muscles coil as he pulls his shirt off, dragging it along and revealing himself to me inch by inch until the shirt is nothing but a crumpled ball of cloth he tosses carelessly on the floor. The way he looks at me, like he wants to devour me, steals my breath.

His barefoot self only in blue jeans making his way to me forces me to take one step back. This man is too much. He has a power over me like no one else.

My back hits the door at the same time his strong hands grab my hips, pinning them there, and his lips meet mine in a heated kiss I've missed for far too many nights.

Everything is hot instantly, my body dying to be touched, begging him to press against me, so I can feel him and only him. I don't want to feel anything else.

His left hand stays where it is, but his right roams up my body, slipping up the curve of my waist, barely touching me and teasing me. All the while my lips part for his deepening kiss, letting him take me as he wants.

With a deft flick of his fingers, he undoes my bra and before the straps can even slip down my shoulder beneath my shirt, his large hand cups my breasts and he moans into my mouth with need. His cock hardened and pressing against my lower belly through the denim of his jeans.

When he pinches my nipple, pulling it ever so slightly, I have to break the kiss to throw my head back. I writhe under him and he doesn't waste another second, pulling me into his arms and taking me to my bedroom, a room he knows all too well.

Even though his gait is large, and his steps swift, he peels the clothes away from me as we go, until I match him in attire.

I can't help but to let out a small squeal of surprise and glee when he tosses me onto my bed. The moonlight peeks through my curtains and that's the only light I have to see him as he kicks off his jeans, along with his boxers and stands in all his glory.

"Pants off," he tells me, stroking himself. The sheen from precum already leaking from him has me licking my lips as I obey. He spreads it around his thick head though, pushing me onto my back even though I got on my knees to lick him.

"Not now, I need to be inside of you," he groans when I mewl in protest. What this man does to me… I just don't know how or why but he plays my body like it was made for him. Bracing himself on top of me, one forearm above my head, he spreads my legs and I spread them even wider in response, tilting my hips for him.

His hand cups my heat and when he presses his palm to my clit, my back arches from the sudden touch and instant desire. "You're so fucking wet for me, baby," his whispers the rushed words out, his lips finding my neck as he pushes two thick fingers inside of me. With his stubble tickling along my neck, his kisses roaming carelessly as he fingerfucks me, the heat inside of me intensifies, burning along my skin and igniting every nerve ending that I haven't felt since he's been here last.

Curving his fingers, he hits that sweet spot inside of me, and rubs my clit with his rough palm at the same time, turning over the waves of pleasure until they finally crash inside of me.

"Dean!" I cry out his name like I need him, like he's the only one I've ever needed as my toes curl and my neck arches with the pleasure rolling through me.

He doesn't wait for me to finish, he doesn't give me a moment to catch my breath. He slams inside of me to the hilt and I scream out in utter rapture. He pistons his hips and it feels like it's too much. My body instinctively curls around his, my legs around his hips as he picks up his pace.

His breath is hot along my neck and every small touch, every deep groan, every thrust from him takes me higher and higher, prolonging the pleasure and keeping me on the edge of falling until he finds his release with my second for the night.

I can't breathe, I can barely move onto my side to close my legs when he leaves the bed to go to the bathroom. The heated waves leave me and the cool air would give me shivers if he hadn't pulled the sheets up around me.

When he comes back, he makes sure I'm alright to fall asleep, before climbing back in.

If tonight is anything like the other nights, he'll have me again in just a little while, and I'll wake up to another round, longer and more gentle, but with just as much pleasure in the morning.

If only I could have him always. If only I knew he wasn't going to leave again…

The thought keeps me from sleeping. It keeps me from feeling the comfort I usually have with him.

Everything just feels out of place. Like something's horribly wrong.

"You're my worst habit," I shake my head, brushing my hair out of my face. I need a shower or even better, a nice long bath with him beside me in that large claw foot tub. But right now, all I want to do is lie here beside him, before he gets up and leaves me again.

"Now I'm a drug?" he chuckles, deep and rough.

"You're a mistake," I correct him, hating the truth that's there. I wish it was only ever a joke. It's not though. The way my heart already hurts and he's not even gone yet… he is a mistake and I know it. I just can't say no to him.

"That's the second time you said that tonight."

Unless I'm mistaken, a hint of his cadence sounds wounded. When I roll over on the bed, still naked and my bare shoulders showing, the sheets roll with me but they don't cover my upper half. A simper dances along my lips when his gaze lowers to my exposed breasts. Part of me wants to tease him, to tell him, *I hope you like the view*. Instead I hold my ground, saying something I've been thinking, every time he leaves me here with only a parting kiss and not even a date when he'll be back.

I whisper, not hiding the pain in the truth, "How could this not be a mistake?" The rustling of the sheets mixes with my words as I lay myself down onto his hard chest, just wanting my skin to be touching his. As if the words I just said aren't going to make him climb out right this second. Contrary to my initial thought, he stays perfectly still. Only for a fraction of a second and I stare at my pillow he's laying against, the masculine scent of him filling my lungs. "You could have a girl like me in every town," I try to joke, to make my voice teasing and force a smile to my lips, but I fail.

"I told you I don't and I don't like you saying that," his voice is hard, but the way his hand comes down around the back of my head, smoothing my hair down is nothing but gentle. "I only have you." Every breath he makes is deep and his chest rises and falls with my cheek on his hot skin. I turn my head ever so slightly, just to kiss his chest. Because a statement like that deserves a kiss at least.

I only have you. It sounds so romantic, but he has me for a weekend and that's all. Then he's gone and I get a call every once in a while, a text here or there, but we're both busy, we live two different lives. The fact that I need to end this weighs on me heavily. This isn't what I want. I don't want a hookup every once in a while. Even if he says all the right things. Even if the smell of him on my pillows lulls me to sleep when he's gone.

"Dean, I--"

"You what, Lysa? You miss me when I'm gone?" he questions me in a tone I don't recognize and it forces me to look up at him. In the depths of his sharp blue gaze there's something there I haven't seen before. Something raw and wounded. "Cause I miss you too. I miss you so much that I don't want to leave."

In this moment, my heart twists. I swear everything stops because my heart can't pump when it's in a knot like it is. There aren't words to fix everything. He asked me once to come with him, to take a vacation and just ride with him. I can't leave the bar though. It's the only piece of my family I have left. It's all on my shoulders.

"I'm tired of missing you," I confess and nearly choke on the words. "I'm too lonely to miss someone who chooses to be gone." His expression doesn't change but his grip on me tightens. I lean forward, needing to be closer to him, praying he understands I just hurt too much when he's gone. My bed creaks with the shift in our weight. "I get it, I do. I swear I understand the family business and--"

Dean's thumb stops me from speaking, pressing it against my lips as his other fingers grace my jaw and he cups my chin, shushing me. I'm not a girl to be shushed though. He leans his head down, in an effort to rest his forehead against mine, but I pull away. I need it to be over. I am addicted to him, but this is killing me.

I think I love you. And it kills me that you don't choose me. It's what I want to say to him. But the words tumble over each other at the back of my throat. My face is hot and my eyes prick with tears and I have to get away and get off this bed to put space between us.

"Lysa, baby, stop," Dean's quick to snatch my wrist, jumping out of the bed and pulling my body against his. He's so much taller, and warmer, every inch of me wants to mold to his masculine form. With soft kisses in my hair, he says something… something that sounds like I love you, but it can't be that.

I try to pull away again, but his strong arm wraps around my waist, pulling me in close again. With both of my palms against his chest, both of us still bared to one another, I'm caught in his heated gaze when he tells me clear as day, "I love you Lysa. And if you'll have me, I want to be here with you. I sold the truck, I left the business. I just want to stay right here with you."

"What?" I'm breathless.

"I sold it, invested the money and I have some left over I thought…" shaking his head, Dean looks past me for a moment then licks his lower lip, his grip loosening on me and vulnerability shining in his pale blue eyes.

"But that's all you've ever known…" the words come out as a murmur.

"No. There's something else I know," he looks down at me with nothing but love. "Something I value more."

"Dean--"

"I thought I could help you with the bar. I don't need you to pay me, you can treat the money like a loan or a gift, whatever you want. I don't need the money, I have enough on my own. I just want to be with you."

Everything blurs around us as the silence passes. Time slows and I know I'll remember this moment forever. I dreamed a thousand dreams over the years, wanting to confess, but he always wanted me to run away with him, like I wanted to do that first time I saw him, back when my father was still here and he would be there to take care of the bar. "Did you say you loved me?" I have no idea how the words manage to escape my lips in a whisper, or where they even came from.

For the first time that I can remember, Dean blushes. With his large hand running down the back of his neck, he grins at me, a boyish grin. "I might have. I might have said I love you so damn much it hurts."

His grin falters slightly until I lift up onto my tip toes to press my lips against his and give him all of me in that one touch.

I don't know when I gave my heart to him, but right now, I vow to give him all of me.

"I love you Dean." I love him so damn much it hurts too. "You promise you'll stay with me?"

Wrapping his arms around me and pulling me into his chest, he brings me back to bed. "I'll stay with you Lysa. I'm here with you. I'm right here. And I'm not leaving anymore."

He repeats, "I love you."

MY SECRET

She's my secret. Mine and mine alone.

SCARLET

I don't pity the men and women who line the bar tonight. As the snow falls behind the paned windows, barely visible with the darkened sky, they lift their glasses. Alcohol drowns out the thoughts of family and friends they aren't with during the holidays. The din of the bar is far from somber though, the occasional laugh ricochets off the paneled walls of this old place.

It may only be a rundown bar off the interstate in the tristate area, tucked away beneath the overpass, but it's warm and feels like home to many. It's my last name on that sign out front. My bar. My home.

It's sure as hell home to me and the only thing I have left from my family. At that thought I peek over my shoulder, a rag in one hand wiping down the glass in the other, and peer at a black and white portrait.

My grandfather always had a Coors Light in his hand and it's there lifted in cheers at the grand opening of this very bar.

That photo, and the occasional postcard from my mother, are all that I have left of my family. She took off when I was five, came back when I was seventeen and my father passed suddenly, but she didn't stay long.

So the sight of Jackson at the end of the bar, his phone always in his hand, and Mr. Richards at the other end, his thinned hair as white as the foam in his beer, feel like home to me. Even on Christmas Eve.

"You're all dolled up tonight," Chrissy comments, her voice is a bit raspy from years of smoking. The stool drags on the floor as she pulls it out to sidle up to her brother.

"This old thing," I respond with a smirk. The deep red shift dress matches a shade of lipstick I put on hours ago. No doubt it's faded by now, but he told me once he loved the color on me.

And I know he'll be here tonight. He told me he would and he's never lied to me. Never let me down.

Chrissy huffs a laugh and then elbows Teddy, saying something about getting out of there so she can hang lights on the tree for her grandkids.

Every minute that passes feels as if it drags for hours. Each beer that hits the bar, every clink of the glass and grinding of the stools against the floor is far too loud.

I'm waiting for one man to walk through that old heavy walnut door.

"Another?" Jackson calls out, lifting his mug in the air and I mindlessly follow suit although my eyes lift to the door at the sound of the chimes.

And there he is.

A warmth spreads through me although I don't show it. My heart pounds and races, my blood heats at the sight of him.

The black flat cap is dusted with snow as he removes it, making his way to the far corner booth. He takes his time slipping off the black wool coat and I only watch him, my gaze shifting from the beer mug filling at the tap to his broad shoulders straining beneath the gray Henley.

In black boots and worn jeans, he sure as hell didn't dress up tonight.

There's a little dance of anxiousness that swells deep in my chest knowing I'm overdressed. "Here you go," I tell Jackson, and don't give him a second look or wait for a response as I make my way to him.

At least I'm in ballerina flats and not heels, but still, heat dances along my skin.

"Your usual?" I offer, my voice wavering as his pale blue gaze reaches mine. He pins me there, the world blurring behind him. Even the air bows down to this man. Dirty blonde hair and a ruggedness tell me he's blue collar, but I know he's more than that.

I've known it for years. He's dangerous. He's a man I once feared. Every instinct told me I should stay far away.

And I would have, I had decided I would.

Two years ago, when I first saw him and he ordered what he'll order now, a gin and tonic, I swore I'd avoid him. It's not just that he looks like a man who's been through hell, that smirk on his lips and that charming smile whisper a secret: he proudly runs the place.

His gaze slips down my body, slowly and deliberately.

In this room that's riddled with onlookers, it feels as if he undresses me. Heat creeps into my cheeks.

"I've missed you," he whispers lowly in a deep baritone that triggers a primal need. It surprises me, he's never said a thing like that until the place is closed up and everyone else is gone.

It's what happens every time. I wait for him and he waits for the bar to close.

And then he takes me however he wants, which is exactly what I crave.

This dangerous man who could do whatever he wishes. He fucks me like I've always been his.

I'm not given a moment to answer, before he nods

and raps his fingers on the old wood table. "The usual."

With a nod, I turn my back to him, my fingers fiddling with themselves until I can grab a tumbler for a gin and tonic.

"You closing early tonight?" Jackson calls out loud enough for the bar to hear him.

With wide eyes, I stare back at him, still reeling from the comment: *I've missed you.*

I nod, without thinking twice, "thirty minutes or so," I tell him. "Snow's getting deep."

The excuse raises Mr. Richard's brow who glances over his shoulder at the devil himself. The man who brought that lie to my lips.

GRIM

The deep red hugs her curves and every inch of her soft skin I've been fantasizing about. It's been over a month, the winter nights getting colder and lonelier without her warmth in my bed.

My cock aches, hard and straining against my zipper as she sways left and right, wiping down the bar.

It's like this every time, she ignores me, just a patron in the corner, as she closes up.

I leave like the rest of them as if she's not the only reason I come to this run down town every chance I get. As if she won't be crying out my name with the strangled pleasure I'll pull from her tonight.

There's no such thing as coincidence. Two years ago I came in here, following a lead and needing a moment to cool down before I did something reckless and stupid.

There she was, staring back at me like I was going to hurt her, like she should fear me.

Smart girl wrapped in a delectable package.

I would have left her alone. Taking another deep gulp of gin, I remember how very much at war I was with myself at the sinful thoughts that plagued me that night.

There's not an ounce of good in me and the things I've done would have her running from me if ever I confessed. But like I said, there's no such thing as coincidence and that night, I craved her. I needed her like I needed the air to breathe.

I waited for her to close down the bar, I followed her, needing to know what the hell it was about her that drew me in.

I heard the footsteps before she did, the clink of the glass bottle being tossed into the trash before some dumb fuck and his buddy catcalled her. Their whistles were sickening.

I'll never forget the look in her eyes, the fear was sobering as she stared at two men who made their way to her. Keys in her hand, she tried to play it off, waving back to tell them to have a good night before she picked up her pace.

All it took was one of them picking up their pace

before I stepped out under the street light, calling out to her.

She stopped where she was, caught right there, my prey, not theirs.

My muscles coiled and I memorized their faces, every detail I needed to find them later, after I'd taken care of my poor little Scarlet.

Caught between the two of them and me, she was paralyzed. They took off when I opened my jacket, letting the light glint off my gun.

"Don't hurt me." The plea was spoken softly as the two pricks left us alone, at three am in the vacant parking lot. "Please," she whispered.

Her hazel eyes shone with more than a prayer for safety.

"You think I want to hurt you?"

"I know you could if you wanted," her response came back without any hesitation.

"That doesn't answer my question." The fear slipped away, quickly replaced with a simmering heat I'd felt from her all night. There's a thin line that separates desire from despair and it had played between us all night.

I lowered my lips to the shell of her ear, the tension crackling between us. "What if I wanted to do something else?"

When I backed away, her eyes stayed closed, her chest rising and falling with heavy breaths. "If you wanted… I imagine you could do whatever you wanted to me."

"Is that you giving me permission?" I murmured in the cold dark night, knowing full damn well I was going to fuck her raw and hard. First against her car, with her breasts pressed against the metal and her skirt barely lifted. And then again back at her place.

This beautiful woman, easy prey and tempting in every way, came on my cock and kept me from making a mistake that night. She may have called me a God that night, but she was my savior.

At first, I felt like a whore. Not in the moment, but after. Once he'd gone and I could still feel him between my thighs, taking me like no man ever had.

Not that I was a virgin, but he was brutal, relentless, he was all consuming.

I slept with a man I didn't know at all. One who chilled me down to the bone, yet with a single look lit every nerve ending inside of me on fire.

He didn't even give me his name or a number. One night, he was mine and the next he was gone. I woke up naked, with both a noticeable ache and disbelief.

All he left behind was a note and a burner phone he must have bought while I was sleeping.

. . .

Use only this phone. My number is in the contacts.

He called himself Grim. I remember laughing when I saw his name under the contacts. There was no way it was his real name, but I liked it. It fit him. It suited what had happened.

The shame came shortly after. When I realized all I had was an old phone and a fake name.

The questions bombarded me and I hesitated to message him. I didn't know what to say or how I felt about what happened.

It was everything and yet I felt like I was left with nothing.

I'd planned on not messaging him at all, but every night, I pulled the phone from the drawer of my nightstand and I debated it. Three nights passed before I sent the first message, if for no other reason than to know the truth.

Are you married? I asked him.

No. I don't believe I ever will be.

It's an odd feeling that came over me, partly relief, partly sorrow.

· · ·

Then why this phone?

I would rather not say. You may ask questions that I won't be able to answer. I have secrets but what I do is to protect you. You need to know that and be okay with some of your questions not being answered.

Over a series of days and messages a number of things became clear.

I was right, he was a dangerous man.

More importantly, which he made clear in no uncertain terms: he wanted me.

And lastly, I wanted him as well.

Every doubt I had, he vanquished. It was as if he knew what I was thinking before I did. From the very moment I felt like what we were doing was wrong, he'd do something to prove I had no reason to worry.

Every night he wished me to dream of him.

Every Sunday he sent fresh red roses.

If I told him I missed him, he would tell me he'd come for me at a certain time, within the next day or so and he was always there. Exactly when he said he would be.

Even if he told me very little, every small secret he confided in me felt like he'd trusted me with his world and I did the same, telling him every secret I had, knowing he'd keep it.

It was like a trance, like some magical spell had been cast. One day this man laid his hands on me, showed me pleasure I didn't know existed and told me I was his.

And suddenly, that's all I was.

My days in and days out hardly changed, apart from my thoughts of him and what he'd do to me when he came back.

It's been nearly every other week for two years now. It's not the romance story for a princess' tale. He's a dark knight with a tortured soul.

I'm not the one who needs saving in this story.

The keys jingle in my hands as I turn the lock and test the door. The harsh night brings a chill that sends shivers down my spine but I welcome the cold.

With the snow crunching beneath my feet I make my way around the side of the bar, to the parking lot where a car is parked next to mine, running but empty. He stands beside it, waiting for me.

Waiting for a night of debauchery with a man who holds secrets and pain I'll never know. A man who craves me and who never leaves me wanting anything but more of him.

He takes three large strides as I near him, eating

up the distance and crashing his lips against mine under the street lights.

With my head tilted back, his hand splayed on my lower back, the other slipping between my legs, I shiver and then moan into his mouth.

His answering groan is sinful as his fingers push past the elastic of my underwear and meet my hot center. He whispers against my lips, "You'd be a liar if you said you didn't miss me too."

GRIM

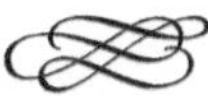

I thought long ago, that whatever was between us would wane. When we first started this, I imagined she would grow tired of it, that I couldn't possibly satisfy her beyond the novelty of a stranger wanting to please her, thoroughly and roughly until her throat was sore from crying out in the dark night.

I anticipated the way she would end it, with a simple request that I would obey. Whether it be because she needed more than I could give her, time and transparency. Or whether it would be because she fell for someone who could provide her with normalcy.

As my thumb rubs soothing circles along the bare skin of her thigh and I drive back to her place, I realize just how addicted we both have become.

She is the only thing I have to look forward to. These moments where I can get lost in her and she can do the same with me. They are the heaven to the hell that is my life.

My scarlet angel.

It's silent in the car for the fifteen-minute slow drive back to her place. The backroads aren't plowed and the snow comes down heavy.

Her hands roam as much as mine do, resting on my jeans but the devilish bit of her reaches up a little higher, feeling my need hard as steel beneath my jeans.

A soft murmur of want slips from her lips but I tell her to wait.

It's agony not to give in right this moment, but I want her beneath me, writhing and struggling not to fight against the pleasure. I want that vision of her so much more than I want those sweet red lips wrapped around my cock.

The moment I park the car, the keys still in the ignition and the car still rumbling, her lips are on mine. Leaning over the console, her lips meet mine with a desperate need.

It amazes me, that a woman like her could want the broken shell of a man I am. I'm quick to push the seat back and pull her into my lap. Her body fits perfectly right here in my arms.

With my hand on her neck, I brush back her long

dark hair from her pale skin and leave opened mouthed kisses there. My other hand pushes aside the silky fabric of her dress and reddens her ass in a demanding grip. She rewards me with a sweet moan I know by heart now.

It's the most blissful sound in my world.

My teeth scrape down her neck, as her head falls back. Nipping and sucking, I leave a trail along her body, but it's far too soon that the cold slips between us.

It's bitter cold and although her house is buried deep in the woods, with the privacy we need, I want her inside, the doors locked and reality a world away.

"Inside," I command her before her pants of need get any heavier.

She crawls off of me, leaving the cold to slip between us, and we both hurry to get inside.

My pulse rages, my cock already leaking precum as she pushes her front door open and I follow her in.

The old house is dark, the floorboards creak and apart from fresher paint, and contemporary décor, the bones and fixtures haven't been touched since the sixties. It speaks to the old souls we have that must've once loved each other.

I don't bother with a light and neither does she. As her shoes fall to the wooden floor in the foyer with a dull thud, I lift her into my arms. A hand on her ass and the other bracing her back.

With a small yelp of surprise and then a soft hum of a laugh, her legs wrap around my hips and her hands find my hair.

Although the back and sides are cropped short, her fingers play and tug at the top of my scalp, giving me just a hint of pain. I fucking love it. Letting out a short grunt of a growl, I nip her neck again, kicking off my shoes and making my way to her small living room.

There's a small fireplace I'll light when I'm finished with her. I've dreamed of laying on her sofa, her back to my front, her hair a messy halo and her cheeks flushed from a night of sin. The fire flickering and crackling as sleep takes us.

That's what I want with her tonight. If I could, I would have her that way every night.

Greedily, my hands roam her body, unwrapping her as if she's a gift fate left just for me. The deep red fabric slips off of her and falls to a puddle on the worn rug beneath my feet.

Her hands slip up my Henley, her fingers running along the divots of my muscles. She plays with me as she likes, as she always does, until I lay her on her back, the sofa groaning with my weight.

She falls easily, bouncing slightly, completely bared to me.

Without hesitation, my lips fall to her breasts and my fingers press inside of her.

Her back arches from the immediate onslaught of sensation and her nails rake down my back. If she wanted to scar me there, leave her mark, I'd gladly let her.

My tongue swirls against her hardened peaks and then I pull back, sucking and plucking her nipples. I'm not gentle and I don't take my time. It's been too long and I'll have all night to savor her, for now, every act is one of a famished man.

Curling my fingers, I press the rough pad of my thumb against her clit and stroke the front of her walls as I finger fuck her pretty little cunt. She's hot and wet, and those sweet little sounds she gives me are everything I've wanted. Her body tenses around me all too soon, and I don't let up, dragging out her release even as she pulses around my thick fingers.

Heat dances along my skin, even if the old house carries a draft. With her, like this beneath me, my world is lit with fire and it blazes between us.

Between sweet murmurs and heavy pants, she pushes her hair away from her face as I stand up and strip. All the while she watches, her small hands drifting down my body along every inch I've kissed myself.

With one knee on the sofa, I lift her legs up, hooking her thighs under my arms and spreading her for me. With a mewl of protest, her hands rest against my chest.

Her lips stay parted but she doesn't tell me no. She doesn't tell me to go easy on her. She wants this as much as I do.

I'm merciless as I slam into her with a single swift stroke. Her breasts press against my chest as she reaches up, clinging to me. I wait a moment, deep inside her, loving how she pulses around me and wait for her to stretch. Taking my time, I pull out slowly, not all the way though and then slam back into her.

She cries out, her head pressing into the sofa cushion and her eyes shut tight. "Please," she murmurs and I do it all again, not knowing what she begs for.

My thrusts come faster and faster, a cold sweat lining the back of my neck as I push her pleasure higher and higher, waiting for the merciful fall.

The sound of me slamming into her over and over combines with our heavy breathing and it fuels me to fuck her deeper and faster. To take her with the primitive need that drew us together from the very beginning.

My toes curl as I fuck her deeper and harder, needing more of her as I get closer to my own release. Not yet. I bury my head in the crook of her neck, grinding the back of my teeth and needing her to come again on my cock before I can even think of giving in.

"Fuck!" she cries out and I mute her cries with a

bruising kiss, not relenting my pace in the least. The sounds that pour from her lips are barely audible as her fingers dig into the cushion, as if she needs something to hold on to.

My heart pounds harder with every thrust.

"Come with me," I command her, my voice strained. Pushing her calf to my shoulder, I angle her deeper and bring my thumb to her clit, ruthlessly rubbing and bringing full on screams of pleasure to her reddened lips.

And that's how we come undone, rushed and desperate, raw and tangled, bared and lost in one another.

With my back to his front, his heavy arm draped over the curve of my waist, we both watch the fire. His lips rest in my hair as he murmurs again how much he missed me, how much he craved this.

It feels as if I am his everything and the words tumble over themselves in the back of my throat: he feels like my everything.

The warmth of the flames lay over my exposed skin until Grim pulls the knitted navy blanket over us. It's barely enough to cover us, and I bury my feet beneath his calves.

There's a rough chuckle that comes from him with the act and then another kiss at my temple.

I could stay forever like this. Not a care outside of

this room. Just wanting to be held by him, all the while, my hand lays over his, our fingers laced.

My heart beats along with his when his phone rings, the sound muffled from his jeans laying over it. The sofa groans as he leaves me, checking it and answers, "Walsh."

There's a pang of pain as he does. With the floorboards protesting his steps that lead him away from me.

I lay waiting, wanting him to come back to me while thinking of the many names others have called him on the other end of that phone.

Cody. Marcus. Walsh.

I asked him once why some people call him Cody and the others Marcus. He said it's because they don't know him and that's the way he wants to keep it.

Before I could pry any further, he told me, I only want to be your Grim.

And I believe him.

Because all I want to be is his scarlet angel.

My throat is dry when he comes back, two tumblers of whiskey from my kitchen in his hand. I accept one and take a deep gulp, letting it burn in a soothing way as he settles back behind me.

"Are they stealing you from me again?" I question him, watching as the fire licks up the log, cracking it and leaving blackness in its wake.

He hums a yes that's deep and allows the regret to linger.

I wonder if one day he'll stay. My fingers slip back around his, his warmth quickly wrapping around me as my cheek falls against his bicep. He pulls me closer and I let my eyes close when I ask him, "How long will they keep you?"

He nuzzles the crook of my neck, the tip of his nose tickling that tender spot before whispering, "not long. I promise."

His hand slips out from under mine, and he grips my hip, startling me as he flips my body over so that I'm on my belly. Hot desire overwhelms me as he tilts my hips up, his erection pressing against my core. A shiver runs down my spine and I hold my breath, wanting him and needing this more than I need anything else. His large frame casts a shadow down on me as he whispers at the shell of my ear, "I want you again."

Thank you for reading this sinful little short. Need more right now? Check out This Love Hurts and get lost in the Merciless World. **For my dedicated readers**, this story takes place AFTER the This Love Hurts trilogy.

LOVE YOU FOR ALWAYS

ANA

He's already dressed, skipping breakfast and heading out the door. Every weekend has been like this. I barely see my husband in the blur of busy days and tired nights.

I wish we could go back to the Golden Coast. To barefoot walks on the sandy beach and times when kisses came easily. Nearly a decade ago, back to the days when Tristan always held my hand. We slept in and cuddled in bed, which always led to more.

Back to the days I was shy to kiss him before brushing my teeth – because back then we would kiss first thing in the morning.

"You're already going?" I ask Tristan as he pours from the pot of coffee into a thermal tumbler with the company logo on it. I blame his work for all of these emotions that keep me up at night, his side of it cold and empty.

Standing in our kitchen, the granite counters clear of clutter except for a single pile of mail, mostly containing bills, and a vase that's been empty since Valentine's day last year, my husband looks up at me. Sympathy echoes in his piercing blue eyes and when he swallow, the cords in his neck go tight. It makes the stubble on his jaw look all the sexier. "I have to Honey." I'll always melt at that nickname.

I'm a sucker for him. He had me the first night he ever laid eyes on me. Tall, broad shoulders that make even a plain white tee shirt look divine on him… I never had a chance with this man.

"I made you coffee though," he offers as if I'd rather have a cup of joe than him. My bare feet pad on the dark gray tiled floors as I make my way to him. They're cold and that makes me all the warmer when he holds me in his arms. Nestling my head against his shoulder, I take in the smell of his cologne, and the feel of his muscular chest as he kisses the crown of my head.

"I wish they'd never sold the company," I say just beneath my breath.

Four years ago, his company sold to another. Nearly everyone lost their jobs. We were the lucky ones because they transferred my husband. He kept his job, but it moved him three states away for most of the week.

My heart squeezes when he doesn't say anything other than, "me too."

I hate how little I see him. I hate that I'm stuck here, with a teaching job I worked my ass off to get, so I barely see my husband. I should be grateful and for a while I was. But distance makes things harder and time can change anything.

"Are you sure you have to go?" I question him when he releases me. I tighten the sash on my robe and fold my arms over my chest.

Years ago, at the Golden Coast, he held my hand on our honeymoon and told me he'd love me forever. I love this man with everything in me, but I don't know how much longer we can survive this.

"I have to. I wouldn't leave if I didn't have to."

My throat's tight when I nod in understanding.

It's a Saturday and I'm in nothing but a robe, while he's fully dressed in a slate gray suit. I want to sleep in and kiss him and love him, to feel him in ways I've desperately been missing. And he says he has to go to work.

"Will you be home for dinner?" I question, finding it hard to keep his questioning gaze.

"Of course," his answer comes out with a careful cadence. Like he knows something's wrong. "You okay?" he questions.

"I miss you," I admit my voice cracking; but he already knows I miss him. It's gotten harder to be away from him, not easier.

"Let me take you out to dinner tonight," he offers. "A date night. Like we used to do."

Hope flutters in my chest, and a smile slips onto my lips until he adds, "I just have a few things to wrap up."

Late nights and constant work comes with who Tristan is. He's always been this way.

"I'll see you tonight then," I answer, closing the distance, getting up on my tip toes to plant a kiss on his lips.

I don't expect his hand to splay on my lower back, keeping me pinned to him or for him to deepen the kiss. But, oh how I love it. His teeth scrape gently against my bottom lip until I part my lips for me, granting him entry. The warmth spreads through me, from my tippy toes all the way up to my cheeks where I can feel a blush blooming.

When he breaks the kiss, he whispers in the way air between us, "Love you for always."

I love him for always too. That's why this hurts so much. It wouldn't, if I didn't love him the way I do.

College is supposed to be where you sow your wild oats, or at least that's what my grandmother used to say. Back then, when I first laid eyes on Tristan at a pub on main street at the university, I thought he'd be a fun time.

And I thought that's all it would ever be.

We burned hot together. The casual glances that held on a little too long, the small touches with the passing drinks as a football game played in the background that neither one of us seemed to care about although the rest of the bar roared with excitement or disappointment every other play.

He was tall, dark and handsome. I was wearing my tightest jeans and a flowy top that gave away a little too much cleavage. I thought the moment he leaned down to kiss me, his lips tasting of pale ale and all male, my hand gripping his bicep through a polo, that we'd have a wild night together. One to remember.

I didn't expect him to call me the next day and tell me he was taking me out that weekend. He didn't even ask me. He later told me, he was terrified I'd say no if he asked. So he took a risk.

That night I wore a red dress, red is supposed to give you more confidence. And a matching shade of red on my lips for lipstick courage. Complete with my best black heels and a little clutch.

That was the first night he told me I looked beautiful.

A week later was the first morning he made pancakes before I woke up and told me I wasn't allowed to sneak out in the morning like I had been.

A week after that, he told me he had feelings. Seeing each other every few days, turned into every other, which turned into us spending fairly equal time, always together, at each other's place.

A month went by before I told him I loved him and he told me he knew, before admitting he loved me too.

I remember it all. Every moment we had. First kiss, first night, first date, first everything.

Each one felt like I wasn't worthy. It's scary to fall in love.

He's the one who said, "I love you for always first."

In the kitchen, at our first apartment together, he brushed his nose against mine while we were making dinner together and he said it.

I believed him because it felt like it was meant to be. Like we were simply made for each other.

My phone vibrates on our bed and I barely hear it, the distant memories of our past still lingering, but I do. As I toss the red chiffon dress onto the bed, I don't know why I was crying. I guess it's the pregnancy hormones and the fact that I don't know how I'm going to tell Tristan. We didn't plan it and I don't know how to tell him. But I have to.

How did we get like this? To the place where we have another first we've both wanted since we got married, but I have no idea how to tell him?

Taking the phone in my hand, I smile at his text: *I'll pick you up at seven.*

TRISTAN

Red is Ana's color.

Something about the shade just suits her. The allure of it, the strength in such a bold choice; she wears it with elegance, even if her fire has dimmed.

As I turn up the radio in the car, it doesn't go unnoticed that she's barely spoken to me. Nervousness pricks its way along the back of my neck. I know she's unhappy and she's been that way, but I'm doing everything I can and tonight I can finally make her happy again.

"You look stunning honey," I compliment her over the hum of the radio.

I still think I have her, she's still mine because every compliment still makes her smile, that beautiful blush coloring her cheeks to be nearly as dark as the clothes she wears.

"You look pretty darn handsome yourself," she whispers and it's then that she places her hand on my thigh as I keep driving. I was waiting for that. Her little touches are everything. I've missed them so much.

With my left hand on the wheel, as I slow at a red light, I lift her hand with my right and kiss her knuckles, one by one, and then turn her hand over, giving her wrist a kiss before the light turns green.

Her small hum of satisfaction and the way her shoulders relax is everything that I needed.

"Where are we going?" she asks me and I tell her it's a surprise but she won't have to wait much longer.

"Oh," she perks up in her seat, a wide smile on her face, "the Blue Grill."

"Our first date as a married couple was here," I remind her.

"How could I forget?" she answers with a smile, her hand still on my thigh as I park the car.

"We sat at the bar because it was so full…"

"My hand may have slipped up your skirt a time or two," I complete the thought for her as I put the car in park and lean over to kiss the crook of her neck. She squeals with delight and I love it. I love everything about her. What we had and, more importantly, everything to come.

We walk side by side, hand in hand through the large double doors of black glass into the elegant foyer of the restaurant.

When I give my name to the host and he leads us to the private backroom, she squeezes my hand and whispers, "What's back here?"

The wooden doors open to a private room, with a single round table in the center, the chairs seated close together. The white table cloth is already laid out with candles, a vase with red roses, and a note on one of the plates. A note I wrote for her.

"Tristan," Ana's voice is tight with emotion and I simply kiss her cheek and pull out her chair for her.

As she scoots in, I take my own seat and rush things more than I wanted to do. I'd planned to make her wait. To wine and dine her like I used to before telling her. But the look on her face, seeing her break down like this, I can't wait. I have to tell her. She's been through enough. These years apart have been so much harder on her and I need her to know that we don't have to do it anymore.

"Read it," I whisper as she stares at the crisp white envelope. "I'm not much of a poet or anything, but I have something to tell you."

She reads the note out loud, her eyes watery, so she dabs them first with the corner of the cloth napkin.

I hope you know I don't take you – or us – for granted.

I miss you every day.

When I said I will love you for always, I meant it because that's all I want to do.

I've only worked so much, to get back home to you.

The moment she reads, back home to you, her hazel eyes widen and she whips her gaze to mine. "What does that mean? You're coming home?" Nervousness and hope wind together in her voice.

Strands of brunette hair fall from the elegant bun on the top of her head. I brush them behind her ear and keep my hand there, cupping her cheek as I tell her.

"I got a job offer in the city. Only forty minutes from our home." Her gasp is covered by her delicate hand. "I've had a few interviews the last few weeks I've been home. That's what I've been doing but I didn't want to tell you. I didn't want to get your hopes up until I knew for sure. I know this has been hard on us and I can't be away from you anymore."

I knew she would be happy, but I didn't expect the tears. I didn't realize she was so emotional about it all.

"I never would have stayed away if I'd known it

made you this upset." At my admission, she shakes her head, reaching out to my cheek and cupping it like I do her.

With the tip of her nose brushing against mine, she steadies herself, giving me a peck on the lips before looking back up at me.

"I'm glad you're coming home because this baby is going to need both of us."

The moment she says baby, her hand moves to her belly and shock and then elation hit me harder than I could ever imagine.

"You're pregnant?" I question her in a single breath and her wide smile is joined with a nod.

I hug her and she hugs me back, both of us clinging to each other, both of us surprised in the best of ways.

There are ups and downs in marriage, there are good times and there are bad, but moments like these and all of our other firsts that we've shared and will share in our lives are so worth every dip on this wild ride.

"I love you," I tell her and kiss her, crushing my lips to hers before she can even say it back.

I love you for always.

FLIRTING WITH A GOOD NIGHT

SYNOPSIS

In our small town, all of my friends have found their soulmates and here I am, moving from one crush to the next but never actually settling down. The reason why is standing only a few feet from me now. He's joking with my best friend's husband, as I sit on their sofa trying not to stare. With his sleeves rolled up, the tattoos he got while he was away in the marines are on display, curved around his toned muscle that flex with his rough chuckle.

Cade was years older and left right after high school. I never told him how I felt, we were so young and there was no way he'd ever go for a sophomore like me. Times have changed and now he's back… and I can't stop staring and pining over the man I've been longing for.

And when he looks my way, with that handsome smirk, rough stubble and gorgeous baby blue gaze…

"Just smell it."

Magnolia's command is murmured with aww, even if it does crack me up. Both of us take a deep inhale that has my back pushing against the cream sectional sofa. Her eyes are closed, her nose just a centimeter above the practically bald little one's head. He has just a small smatter of dark brown hair at the very top of his noggin and with the little jostle, he coos, putting a wide-eyed Autumn on edge.

"There's nothing like it in the whole world." Magnolia's statement is met with both another coo from Cameron, the two-week old little one fast asleep in her arms, and a long exhale of relief from his mother. Autumn's arms are still up as if she was getting ready to snatch her newborn and quickly rock him back to sleep if he woke from the two of us taking a nice long whiff of that baby smell.

I bite back my smile, unable to not see the humor in the room with Magnolia completely missing Autumn's stress.

"Seriously," Mags presses, "There's something about the way they smell…" I finally let out a laugh when Mags closes her eyes and lays back with the little boy.

"If you keep creeping me out, I'm taking my baby back," Autumn's response is given with a broad smile. You'd never know she just went through almost thirty hours of labor earlier this week.

There really is something about that sweet baby powder like scent, though. I have to agree with Mags, pulling my legs up on the sofa and then resting my pointer against Cameron's little cheek. "He is freaking adorable Autumn," I murmur and feel my heart swell with happiness for her and Trent and their other two boys.

"I want another baby." Mags cradles the baby closer and Autumn's eyes go wide.

"If you wake him, you keep him," she comments while dragging the basket of clothes across the kitchen island to be closer to her. She's all the way at the end of it, now perched on a stool, while the two of us, strike that, two and a little a bundle, are huddled at the end of her sofa where the living room meets the kitchen.

Our Wine-down Wednesdays have certainly changed recently. Mags with her … shall I say love life dilemma, and Autumn with her ever-growing family.

"I'm not going to wake him up," Mags admonishes Autumn then makes an 'oops' expression as Cameron wiggles in her arms.

The little man has only been on this earth for less than 2 weeks but he knows how to make the whole world stop as he nestles in tighter.

"I would steal him away from you," I start and then we all hear the front door open and the sound of several boot steps filter in through the house. "But I have to get going," I finish as the sight of two men interrupts the conversation.

With a charming smile, the first man pauses to cup the little one's head. Giving me the perfect comparison of father and son.

Cameron looks just like Trent, Autumn's husband. His little nose and those large brown eyes. They are all Trent.

With a pout from Mags, and her pulling the baby into her arms playfully, as if to say 'he's mine, off,' Trent chuckles and makes his way to Autumn, planting a kiss on her cheek before setting down a number of plastic bags on the counter next to his wife.

What is it with men and carrying every single bag from the grocery store in at once?

"Thanks for giving him a ride while his car is in the shop," Autumn's gratitude is met with a little nod from the second man.

The one who has my heart stuttering from my place on the sofa.

"No problem," his deep voice echoes and I take the chance to drink him in.

In our small town, all of my friends have found their soulmates and here I am, moving from one crush to the next but never actually settling down. The reason why is standing only a few feet from me now. He's joking with my best friend's husband, as I sit on their sofa trying not to stare. With his sleeves rolled up, the tattoos he got while he was away in the marines are on display, curved around his toned muscle that flex with his rough chuckle.

He was years older and left right after high school. I never told him how I felt, we were so young and there was no way he'd ever go for a sophomore like me. Times have changed and now he's back… and I can't stop staring and pining over the man I've been longing for.

And when he looks my way, with that handsome smirk, rough stubble and gorgeous baby blue gaze… Lord, have mercy.

"Cade Jameson," Magnolia calls out as she gently

sets the infant down for the first time since she snatched him from me. The little bundle lays effortlessly into the rocker at our feet.

With a gentle touch, I rock the little one, still bundled in a 'choo choo', blue plaid, train swaddle and look anywhere but at the man who's become the center of conversation.

In my periphery, I gauge the friendly hug between them. It's nothing more than polite. Well maybe a touch comical considering how short she is and how he has to bend down to hug her in return. She's a bit petite and Cade is a wall of muscle, taller than most.

"It's good to have you back. You staying long?

"I am," he answers proudly and I only notice that I'm staring, waiting with baited breath for his answer, when his gaze lifts past Mags to where I am.

I'm quick to look away although I continue to eavesdrop about how he'll be home through the holidays and how he's stationed here now, hopefully permanently.

My little heart pitter patters at the thought of him being back home for good.

"You staying for dinner?" Autumn questions and it takes me far too long to look up and realize she's asking me.

"Oh, no. I have to head out and I already ate." I answer her but then realize once the words were spoken that she already knew that. I told her the moment I got here and stole Cameron from her before Magnolia could.

"You're walking home?" she questions further, the room of eyes on both of us. I ignore the heat that comes with Cade's prying gaze.

"That's how I got here," I cock a sarcastic brow Autumn's way and wonder why she added concern to her tone. I always walk to her house, she knows that. It's one of the reasons I love this neighborhood so much. As I stand, I stretch out my back slightly, focusing on the cream throw I'm folding rather than the man whose gaze is falling down my body.

Years ago I thought the tension between us was imagined. Or at least one sided. But this is the third time I've seen him since he's been back and I swear it only gets more and more obvious that I can't keep my eyes off of him and I know he does the same. Stealing glances each time we've had a run in together.

"Why doesn't Cade take you home?" Autumn offers, folding a tee-shirt in her lap and then adding it to a pile on the counter.

Oh, the betrayal. She doesn't have the decency to look me in the eyes. Instead she focuses solely on Cade as my heart completely halts in my chest. "You can take her home on your way, can't you Cade?"

Alone with this man? In his truck? Late at night with my ovaries still doing flip flops at the sight of a newborn?

Oh, no, no, no.

"Of course I can," he answers easily, a touch of southern hitting his last word as he slips his hands, which I already know are rough from years of manual labor, into his jean pockets. His asymmetric smile greets me, "Ready when you are, Shar."

Shar. It takes great effort not to swoon just from the way he says my nickname.

CADE

There's nothing like the autumn leaves, hues of gold and red, being carried down the gravel road of this old town. Or the smell of the apples and the laughter of kids playing at the edge of the orchard that lines this half of the neighborhood I grew up in.

Nothing like the soft sigh that comes from Shar's plump lips either or the way the wind blows her brunette locks as I help her into my truck.

It's all a part of home to me. A home I missed dearly for years.

Her hand is small in mine and the blush that rises up her chest and into her cheeks is certainly from my hand on the small of her back rather than the chill in the air. I've always had an effect on her, one that forces a hint of a chuckle from me and she peeks up through her lashes and then finds her place in the passenger side.

"Thank you," she whispers shyly, letting me shut her door after giving her a small nod and a "no problem."

Shar has no idea how much I thought about her while I was overseas. How the stories Trent would tell me, keeping me up to date on this town, always seemed to come back to her.

It didn't matter what news was filtering through the town gossip, I needed to know about her and what she was doing, if she was with anyone. I had no right, she doesn't even know how I feel about her, but there was a piece of me that needed to hear she was doing alright without me.

Coming home every so often and catching up with a beer and friends was never complete until Shar idled in. Her confidence hitching just like her breath did every time she saw me.

I felt it, whatever it is that crackles between us now, but I never acted on it because it would only be days until I was gone again.

That changes now though.

The truck rocks gently as I pull my door shut after helping her get in on her side.

"You know you don't have to," Sharon speaks

first as I bring the truck to life with a rumble and turn down the music so I can hear her caressing voice that much better. "I could walk."

My window's already rolled down and I set my elbow there, resting my chin in my hand, my pointer running along the rough stubble of my jaw as I stare at her and wait for her to look back at me.

"I like the opportunity to be a gentleman when I can be."

"Mm," she murmurs. "You imagine you're some kind of gentle beast, huh?" she jokes, but there's a breathlessness to her taunting. Both of her hands find her lap and then fall between her knees, which makes her thighs part.

A gentle beast? I'm not so sure of that. Not with the thoughts running through my mind right now. Imagining how I'd part those thighs of hers, barely covered by her burgundy cotton dress.

"I might be all brute, I think," I comment back, half-jokingly. "But I at least try."

She laughs gently, her chest rising and falling easily. With her hair swept across her shoulder she leans back, closing her eyes and listening to the faint music.

"Well thank you, Cade."

My cock twitches just from her saying my name. It's too rough a word for her seductive lips. Readjusting, I put the car in drive.

"Blue house on the corner, right?" I ask her and she nods.

"Right across from the lake."

"Yeah I remember now. It's been a year since."

"Since you dropped me off when I was wasted?" she questions and shakes her head, her beautiful gaze on the auburn leaves that blow in the wind as we drive by. "Thank you for that by the way… It was not my best night."

"We were all wasted," I attempt to appease her. If I was being fully honest, I'd admit to her that I'm glad she was too far gone that night. My fingers itched to hold her and if she'd been more sober, I'd have leaned in for a kiss. I'd have wanted more. Only for me to be called away the very next day. It was meant to happen, to give us more time for when it'd be right.

A time like now.

I lay my forearm on the center console, daring to get a little closer to her, my hand only inches from her.

"Seriously, thanks for that night. It was …"

"A good night," I stop her from finishing the word 'embarrassing.' "I love coming home and getting to hang out with you." I almost say 'you guys,' but I cut it off deliberately, choosing not to hide anymore. Not to hold back.

"Oh, is that right?" Shar swallows thickly, the

sound of it bringing my attention to her slim throat and the dip just beneath it that begs me to lay an open kiss right there.

With the heat climbing in the cabin, no matter that our windows are both open, I pull up in her drive and park the truck. "You like hanging out with me?" she asks, a hint of reverence playing in the sweet cadence of her question.

I can only nod, my grip slipping slightly on the wheel as my palms turn sweaty.

"I like the way you look at me," I push her gently, calling her out and finally being a man when it comes to her and what's between us.

"I look at people, yeah," she tries to play it off.

"You blush the same way too? When you look at other people."

I'm only given a deeper hue of red as she sits in that seat, biting down on her lip. A lip I'd like to suck while my hand roams between her legs. I have to shift in my seat and I notice she squirms in hers too.

The crickets and nightlife are the only backdrop as I turn the keys in the ignition and let the silence take over.

"You don't make me blush, Cade," she lies and then stares out her window to correct herself. "Well... you make all the girls blush so it's not the same."

"I don't notice it with other women. I don't notice anything about them."

"Now you're just trying to prove a point and make me blush," she accuses.

"Tell me you didn't look at me different from the other guys?" Damn, it's odd how much thinking that's a possibility hurts. The pain vanishes the second Shar looks up at me with wide eyes.

"I feel like you always did," I admit.

Her breathing is shallow and her lips slightly parted.

"Do you want to come in?" is all she says, her fingers digging into the leather of the seat beneath her, as if she has to cling to it to keep her seated there.

"And why do you want me to come in Shar?" I don't know why I tease her, why I prolong the tension, other than that I need her to admit it too.

"Because I don't want to be alone tonight?"

"You answered that like you were asking another question."

Her gaze drops and insecurity flashes in her gorgeous eyes.

"Come on, Shar. Tell me the truth. Tell me all of this isn't in my head and something I just made up."

My heart rages against my chest and my pulse races, waiting for her to answer.

She shakes her head gently, swallowing first, and then admitting, "If you mean the fact that I've wanted you for years and that I've dreamt what could have happened that night a year ago… then no. It's not in your head."

"Then, yeah, I want to come in."

His lips were on me so fast, his hands on my waist, pinning me against his truck. The only reason my eyes aren't closed as he devours me is because I need to see it, to know I'm sane, and that this all isn't a dream.

Cade Jameson, the boy who stole my heart in high school and left with it for years is back a man, demanding the very thing I've wanted since I first laid eyes on him.

With his large hands at my hips, his lips drifting down my neck and the chill of the autumn night air leaving goosebumps along my exposed skin, I can barely breathe, let alone believe this is real.

It's the site of my neighbor, Miss Clare Jane peeking through her blinds that snaps me out of the haze.

All hot and bothered, I'd feel shame if I wasn't living out a fantasy I'd trade all my modesty for in a heartbeat.

"Cade, inside," I whisper at the same time he rakes his teeth up my neck and smiles at the shell of my ear.

He whispers, "You have no idea how long I've dreamed about doing just this." His grip on me loosens and with a gentle hand in mine, helping me find my balance, he leaves a kiss just beneath my ear and adds, "But I was more of a brute than a gentleman in those dreams, Shar."

Pulling back, he gives me a charming smirk, "I'll mind my manners until we get through that front door of yours."

Oh, my... not a single word can finish that sentence. None come to mind even.

All the heat that had gathered between my legs burns its way up my body as I somehow find the ability to walk at a seemingly normally pace to my front door.

I'm already on edge just from knowing he wants me. Just from that short moment he had me pinned.

His strong hand wraps around mine, his deft fingers slipping against mine and caressing in soothing circles as I open the door.

The chill behind me isn't from the night air, it's from his immediate absence as I walk in and turn in my foyer, the light from the porch shining a light on his hulking body as he stands in the doorway.

"I have to apologize," he starts and with a quick intake, my heart betrays me, squeezing tight at the thought that he isn't going to come in. But then he does. A single step and then another. Each one of his, is met by one by me, luring him deeper in the house, until my back is pressed against the wall and the front door closes with a resounding click.

"I swear next time I'll lay you down right," he whispers although his words scream in my head, the lust making the quite polite words sound dirty. It's his hungry gaze that seems to tear my clothes off even though he's not touching me. His careful steps as if I'm his prey when he's aware I'm willingly already his.

"But tonight, I have to do this," he finishes the thought that seems to take forever to complete all the while my body heats and the desire takes over.

He's on me in an instant, my back arching from the intensity of his kiss. His lips press against mine as his hands roam down my body, lifting up my skirt and pushing my underwear aside.

My lips mold to his and I moan in his mouth as his thick fingers brush against my swollen nub and then drift lower, through my slick folds and to my heated core. He groans, his head falling back for a moment before he rests his forehead against mine. His lids are still closed and I stare up at him, my heart racing, needing more. My entire being depends on the words that are sure to fall from his lips.

"You're so fucking wet for me," he comments with reverence and before I can respond, I'm in his arms, my legs wrapped around his hips. With my back against the wall, he balances me there, his left hand pulling at the strap to my dress which falls carelessly, seemingly also affected by the unfair spell he's always had over me.

If I could speak, I'd tell him that. I'd admit I've been ready for him for longer than he knows. I'd confess how much I want him, if only every nerve ending wasn't lit along my skin, making his harsh touch filled with desperation ignite a craving both of us need to satisfy this very instant.

"Cade," I cry out his name as he rakes his teeth down the curve of my neck and pulls my dress down lower, taking my bra strap with it until I'm exposed to him.

"I promise next time I'll give you more attention," his calm words, force the haze of want to subside for only a split second, just enough to hear the unzip of his jeans. Then I'm gone, gone far away and higher than I've ever been with my lips dropped into the perfect "o" as he fills me in a swift motion, his thick length stretching me.

With my heels dug into his ass, my body freezes,

paralyzed by the sudden wave of pleasure that holds me hostage.

"I'll give you time," he groans against my neck, still buried deep inside of me. My thighs tremble around his hips, my core stretching to accommodate his size.

"This is how I pictured it," he murmurs and I half wonder if he's telling me, or confessing a sin. "This is exactly how I've wanted you," his rough timber vibrates against my heated skin.

If I could speak, I'd admit the same, but he rocks just then, his pubic hair pressing against my clit and sending a moan to take over the words I dared to utter.

His lips find mine again as he rocks in and out, a gentle beast for a moment, before his pace picks up. My fingers dig into his skin, raking down his back and I find myself clinging to him, surrounded by his masculine scent. He fucks me, hard and rough until I have to silence my screams by biting down on his shoulder. The sudden movement awards me with a deep rumble of a groan that spurs him on. Faster, harder, relentlessly until I'm crashing hard against the wave of my release and he's doing the same.

He's gentle when he sets me down, although my legs are weak.

My head's dizzy and my body's numb all too

soon. The climax still wracking through my body and leaving me so limp I nearly fall to the floor.

Nearly, but I don't. Disbelief still forcing me to have some semblance of grip on reality.

I just slept with Cade Jameson… No, no, Cade just fucked me against the wall of my foyer. They're two very different things and all I want from him now is *more*.

"Do you want to stay?" I dare to ask him, not even waiting to catch my breath. "You want to stay with me tonight?"

Cade lifts his gaze to mine as he pulls up his jeans, buttoning them and already appearing put together. It's not fair, because he's left me shattered and I know I look the part.

I'm a well fucked mess and his tussled hair shows the evidence of what I've done to him, but nothing else does.

Insecurity wraps its way around my heart until he speaks.

"I'm a pretty easy-going guy, Shar. This could be one good night. It could stay between us. It could be more."

Leaning against my foyer wall, still feeling him inside of me, it takes everything for me to believe this really happened. It's happening right now.

"I want it to be more, but that only matters if you want that too. So you tell me." Vulnerability shines in his light blue eyes when he asks, "You want me to stay?"

If you loved this sexy little short, you'll devour the first novel in this small town romance world. Start reading Tequila Rose today!

THE THINGS YOU DO TO ME

CHAPTER 1

Aria

The snow falls slowly, drifting in the wind along the once-dark tree line. With the blankets of snow covering every inch that I can see from the large kitchen window, everything shines brightly.

Parting my lips, I close my eyes and down the last bit of sweet red in the stemless wine glass. I've never been fond of the cold, but this ache in my chest today… it's not from the feet of snow that keep us locked inside the house.

"He's out there," I whisper, feeling the brooding shadow of the man I call my husband behind me.

"Yes, songbird, our son is out there and just fine."

With my long hair falling from my shoulder I turn around to face Carter. "When are they going to be home?"

With all of his hard features and dark gaze, Carter still manages a smirk that lights a fire in the pit of my stomach. It rages for him to deny the fact that our son is still young and last night was the first night he spent away from us. And now it's snowing… feet of snow.

"Chloe said he's having fun."

A sigh leaves me and a part of me knows that ache in my chest is because my little baby boy is growing up. He's on the move and wanting to play.

I miss the late-night cuddles and the way Anthony used to wrap his chubby little fingers around my pointer.

"I just wish I could see him…" I comment, making my way to the large polished counter where, upon inspection, the wine bottle I was going to get is now empty.

"You didn't want to go. Miss 'I don't love the cold.'"

I stare down at my glass as if it's a traitor and somehow it swallowed up my wine before I was able to drink it.

Two large hands grip my shoulders tenderly.

Carter's thumbs rub soothing circles along the blades of my upper back and then higher, where they dig in deeper, soothing my sore muscles.

With his lips at the shell of my ear, he whispers, "You're stressed."

I swallow thickly and admit, "I know."

"You're a good mother and he's in very capable hands."

"The house is empty…" I stress. Everyone else left to enjoy the snow. This house, typically filled with the sound of so many family members, is now silent.

"Yes," Carter's voice deepens. Moving his lips to the crook of my neck, he lets them fall and lays a kiss right there, sending a pulsing wave of desire through me. My back to his chest, he pulls me in closer and I drop the empty glass to the counter, bringing my hand up to run my fingers up the nape of his neck as he kisses me again and then says, not hiding the lust, in the shell of my ear, "We have the house to ourselves. We should take advantage of that."

Carter

My worrying wife is beautiful. She's always radiant and poised. When that soft smile hits her lips, life itself seems to melt away into nothing but peace. That's what this woman gives me: a life I never thought I'd have, let alone deserve. One I want to share with her forever. I'll give her everything to keep that smile that lingers on her wine stained lips in place, right where it belongs.

"Let's get you another bottle…" As I take a step back, my songbird places her small hand in mine, letting me lead the way. After three years together, there's no fight for power, no resentment at the way we came to be. I led her away from a pain and darkness that kept her trapped and she did the same for me. There is only love that remains and from me, a gratitude I'll forever be in debt to her for giving to me.

In a dark blue, silk to the touch nightgown she glides to the wine cellar door, opening it with a soft creak, but only inches before turning on her heel in her bare feet to look up at me.

"Cross," her voice turns tempting, with a hint of sin that dances from her tongue. "Are you trying to get me drunk?"

A deep chuckle rises from my chest and the hint of a smile lingers on her lips… "*Mrs. Cross,*" I emphasize her name and remember a time when the idea of me responding in that way would have been an impossibility. A time when she called me 'Cross' out of pure resentment for who I was. "That goal is a little too easy to achieve for a man like me," I tease her back, watching the simper on her beautiful face grow as the blush rises from her chest to her cheeks and she shyly looks away.

With a swat of her hand against my broad chest, Aria shakes her head. "Well if he's not coming home tonight and we're making the most of this," she speaks as she peeks up at me through her thick lashes, "I think I'll have one more glass."

My hand splays along her back and I pull her in close to me, feeling her warmth and softness curve around me. She gasps when I nip her exposed shoulder, "Well go get it then."

Aria

The cellar door closes with a click and with only the dim illumination, Carter's brooding frame takes up too much of the light.

"I can manage to grab a bottle," I tease him and make my way to the back of the cellar and to the right. The wine cellar is far too much, with four rows of wine lining the aisles from floor to ceiling and a bricked floor made to look worn, hints of brown matching the dark wood and iron accents in the space that's much larger than most bedrooms. I love it though.

"You could," Carter starts as I round the back corner, aiming for a section of Cabernet that Addison and I are both fond of. My breathing halts when I see the cream throw blanket laid out on the floor. Two glasses of red are already poured, waiting next to the blanket and chocolate covered strawberries are piled in a balanced stack on a silver tray. "Or we could make the most of tonight."

Carter's whispered answer forces me to turn from the scene and stare up at the man I love so dearly.

Taking one step closer to me, he asks, "Do you remember that spot? When you were first here and what you told me, drunkenly as you stared up at me wanting things to change?"

Tears prick my eyes and I shake my head. I try not to remember those times if I'm honest. I don't tell Carter that, I only shake my head. It's not often my Beast turns into a Prince. This is so unexpected, so sweet and it takes me by complete surprise.

"I don't."

An asymmetric smile picks his lips up, "It doesn't matter, really, what matters most is that I never wanted you to leave. And now I have you forever."

Shaking off the wave of emotions, I gaze into his

dark eyes watching the flecks of gold that brighten when I smile up at him. "Forever and always," I whisper as I get on my tiptoes to plant a kiss on his lips.

There's a groan that escapes when I lean back just slightly. A deep sound of approval but also of want.

"Lay on your back and close your eyes," he gives the command with his own eyes closed. Restraint showing in the way he lets go of me and his body goes still, waiting for me to obey.

I don't hesitate, quickly finding my spot on the already smoothed out throw blanket. With a slight chill in the air, my nipples are already hardening. I'm careful not to knock the glasses or tray as I lay down, and wait.

Anticipation rolls through me, from my toes up to my neck and then higher, forcing my breathing to come in faster.

"Dessert tonight is going to be exquisite," Carter comments as he pulls the button-down shirt over his head, only unbuttoning the first few. He's eager. In past times he's made me watch as he's undone every button, showing off his taught skin and muscles that coil beneath the expensive fabrics of his shirts and suits. Not tonight.

Tossing the shirt behind him carelessly, he comes closer, taking his time to round my body but never taking his eyes off of me, as if I'm his prey. He takes more time undoing his pants and letting them fall along with his boxers. Towering above me, naked and with a deep hunger etched in his expression, my heart picks up its pace, no longer wanting to stay where it should. The *thump, thump, thump* heats my entire body.

He kneels at first, letting his deft fingers linger on my collar and then slipping down the strap to my nightgown. He exposes one breast, groaning once again that deep primitive sound, before sliding the remainder of my nightgown down to my hips. He pauses then, dipping his head between my breasts and letting his tongue run hot circles along my tender skin. He bites down ever so gently around my nipple and my back arches involuntarily.

"Still, songbird," he commands, not lifting his head and only pausing in the torturously pleasurable act enough to remind me that I'm to stay still.

I already know, but my body doesn't obey. It takes focus to ignore the need to writhe under him as he plays with my body. His fingers just barely touching my skin as he glides his hands down my curves and removes the garment completely.

Still on his knees he rakes his gaze along my body, balling the silk fabric and then dropping it to be nothing more than a puddle on the floor behind him. Naked beneath him, I should be cold with the chill of the cellar, but I'm hot and greedy for more.

He takes his time, leaning over me, but not touching a single inch of skin to mine to take the first chocolate covered strawberry.

"One small bite," he demands, tracing the tip of it along my bottom lip. The chocolate is sweet and decadent as I bite into it and the strawberry even sweeter. It's heaven on my tongue.

But what Carter does next is even more delightful. Letting the bitten part of the berry travel down my skin to leave a trail of juice in its wake, he licks behind it. Starting at the tender under-side of my chin and working his way down my neck and chest, the cool touch of the berry is quickly followed by his hot tongue. When he gets to my breast, he pauses placing the strawberry at my lips again and once again I take a small bite, but he commands me to take a larger one and so I do. As I swallow, he finishes off the fruit and takes another, repeating the act over and over, half a dozen times, causing every nerve ending in my body to spark.

He works me up, but never finishes me, never touches the one place I ache the most for his mouth to linger.

"Tell me what you want songbird," he commands, the last strawberry in his hand as he stares down at me.

"I want you," I beg him and even to my own ears I sound as if I'll die if he doesn't enter me right this second. My hands clench at my sides, hating that I can't simply take from him, but knowing it's so much better if I'm patient.

"Don't bite it," he tells me, sliding the strawberry halfway into my mouth. I keep my gaze on him as his broad shoulders travel lower, his strong hands gripping my inner thighs to part them. He settles between my legs, his shoulders propping up my thighs until the balls of my feet are on the floor. His warm breath trailing along my most sensitive area.

He takes one languid lick of my pussy and my head falls back from the wave of pleasure.

"That sound," he groans at my heat, "I fucking love it when you make that sound." With the statement still in the air, my sex-driven mind slowly comprehending his words, Carter sucks on my clit, massaging his tongue against it and I disobey him, biting into the berry and pushing myself into his face.

He grips my ass, pinning me down and continues to suck and lick and dive his tongue inside of me as the waves build and the pressure mounts and then finally, all at once and so much faster than I expect it to, pleasure erupts inside of me. Rolling from the tips of my fingers down my body and back up again.

With my heavy breathing making my chest rise and fall, I stare up at Carter, ready to apologize for biting into the berry. But he doesn't give me the chance.

My beast of a husband parts my legs wider and thrusts himself inside of me without warning, to the hilt. My palms hit the ground as my back bows and the orgasm I thought had subdued rages inside of me, growing hotter with every pounding thrust of his hips.

"Carter!" I scream out, feeling the overwhelming loss of control as he pistons himself inside of me.

"Yes," the word falls from his lips as a hiss and he drops his body to lay across mine, although his forearm, braced above my head, supports his weight. "Cry out for me, Aria. Scream my name."

Losing all sense of control, my heels dig into his ass and my hips tilt, letting him fuck me deeper and harder as I scream out his name like he told me to and like everything inside of me wants to do.

He's ruthless and relentless as he takes me, fucking me until we find our release together.

Lying beside him, I wince when I turn over, still feeling him inside of me. "I bit the strawberry." I whisper and the small admission awards me a chuckle from the spent man beside me. Deep and masculine and everything Carter is.

With a wicked smile he stares down at me, "I'll prepare for your punishment tonight."

I can only smile back, so aware that it would be impossible not to keep the strawberry where it was while he did what he did to me. He can play these games, he can lead me wherever he deems fit, and I will follow loving every step of the way.

"I love you Carter Cross."

"And I love you, my songbird."

To experience Carter and Aria's story from the beginning, read Merciless today!

A SINGLE NIGHT

A bonus scene from Jase & Bethany's Irresistible Attraction Trilogy

CHAPTER 1

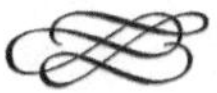

"*D*oes it scare you?"

Does it scare me? Does the fire licking along my skin scare me?

Not like he scares me. It's not a fear of who he is or what he could do to me. The fear is deeply rooted in the knowledge that I lose myself around him. That the background fades to blackness and all I can see is his masculine physique.

"No," I dare to whisper. It's so quiet in the vacant room, that all I can hear is the click and then the hiss of a tender flame that grows larger and then brighter, the lit candle coming to life.

Stripped down to nothing, lying against the leather, I wait for him with baited breath.

My skin is already sensitized, the edge of knife he used to shave down my body made sure of that. The blade glints from the simple steel cart behind him. Everything he needs for his fire play hides away in that drawer.

"Not like it did at first," I admit a truth and the innocence of it doesn't escape me.

With the candle in his right hand, his left caresses the pinkish skin of my waste. "Even if there was so little, it would singe," he speaks as he trails his fingertips from the curve, up to my belly and then lower.

He prefers a knife to a razor and a candle for a flame. First he strips me, leaves me here in the chill of his absence, and then it begins.

As his fingers slip lower, past my belly and even farther still, his satisfied groan disrupts the heavy breathing that's lingered between us. "Already wanting me," he comments as the tip of his blunt nails slip down my most sensitive nub.

"Part of me wants to be selfish." His tone is even, deep and with the soothing cadence that calms me. His thumb slowly, teasingly, spreads me and then moves back to that most sensitive place, where he spreads my arousal. The spike of heat and want stir in the pit of my stomach, the desire escaping me in a gasp that parts my lips. "Part of me," he continues as he reaches for the ethanol, "doesn't even want to play tonight."

My voice is strained and it takes great effort to open my eyes and meet his soft gaze. I swear the vulnerability that shines in the bright light of the flame wasn't there days ago. It echoes back to me now, making my throat dry as I remind him, "Whatever it is, the clock is running."

Wherever the alcohol is placed, the flame will dance. The fuel of it, the trail placed on my skin, dries so quickly, licked clean by the bright light, that it's only a flash. Only a moment of the heat that threatens to burn.

The air between us thickens and the flame drops and the bead of wax drips slightly. Gripping the table harder, my back arches and the sudden heat is met with my moan.

"You're … needy, wanting..." Parting my closed I catch sight at his tongue darting across his lower lip. "Tempting… I imagine I could blow, and you'd reach your limit, wouldn't you?"

As he walks to the end of the table, letting the wax melt as he goes, allowing it to drip carelessly, recklessly down my already sensitive skin I wonder if he'll do it. I wonder if it's all too much for him like it is for me and he'll take me now like my body begs.

I don't know at what point the need changed, but it's as if it's all different now. At least in this moment. Locked in this barren room for him to do as he wishes to me. I don't know when it happened… but everything has changed.

"Tell me what you want?" he murmurs, his lips

brushing against my inner thigh, his warm breath giving me just enough, to stop the chill of goosebumps from taking over. With no heat, not a single bit of it, my body aches for the void to be filled.

The flame and the wax aren't enough.

With a single low breath, he blows against my core and then higher. My lips stay parted and I'm fully aware my expression gives it all away. The arch of my back as the tenderness of a burning need sends me higher.

"I need an answer," he murmurs his left hand gripping my right thigh and as he holds me still, dripping the wax at the same time that a languid lick sends my orgasm over the edge.

"You," the word is begging, desperate even, as it's torn from me.

The spike of my release has barely waned before he's ripped me from where I lay and positioned me, a fist of my hair at the base of my neck, the candle recklessly dropping to the floor.

He enters me without warning, swift and ripping a strangled moan from my throat. I don't recognize myself or my own voice as he takes me, my back to his chest. The fingers of his other hand gripping my hips and the relentless thrusts deepened by my hips pinned to the table. With no place to go, I'm his to ravage and that's exactly what he does. My nipples pebble, the cool air no match for his skin scorching my back.

He's rough … but only for so long. Only until I'm limp, the pleasure rocking through me, taking from me, draining my strength to do anything but call out his name in mercy as my body sags against the warm leather.

....

With his lips trailing down my neck, he parts them ever so slightly, and a trail of goosebumps linger where his gentle touch has been. The intensity of such a gentleness, brings the onslaught of my climax higher and my back arches as he finds his release. His rough groan of utter satisfaction is accompanied with a final thrust that he holds deep inside of me, forcing even more from me, more than I can handle. My nails dig in his corded forearms, in a weak attempt to stay grounded as we both fall from the highest high and my orgasm crashes around me, like the burning rubble of a fixture engulfed in blistering flames.

My chest rises and falls recklessly with my heavy breath as reality slips back. The table groans as he readjusts, and I expect him to leave me, and for the chill to settle in. Instead he braces himself on his forearms and places a kiss just beneath the tender spot beneath my ear. He whispers, "Bethany," softly and with a delicate cadence that brings the goosebumps back, beginning where the word was breathed and slowly trailing down every inch of my sensitized skin.

Even though there are moments I despise his entire being and the part he's played in my pain and other moments where the intensity of what he could do to me and what I'm all too aware he's done in the past chill me to my core, I can't deny there's a tenderness now. There's a scorched section of my twisted heart that has been scarred and branded. Not from his harshness, no, he scarred me with this side of him, the side that brings out a pain and longing I've never felt before.

I find my lips parting with my gaze caught in his and I whisper with the same reverence his just held, "Jase."

Until the debt is paid, I am his.

I am so happy I can sit on my rear and write sexy stories for you guys! I hope you enjoyed this alternative scene from my A Single Glance trilogy. Jase and Bethany's complete story is available now, start reading with A Single Glance.

BEAUTY & THE BEAST

PROLOGUE

Calum

"Sir, are you sure you want to do this?"

Alessio's hesitation is personified by weakness.

It was different when I started. We were all different back then, and I know my driver longs for the days where my reputation didn't send shivers of ice down the back of spineless men.

Maybe I'm more callous than I once was when wealth flowed freely, and my partners held more respect for me than they did fear. That's what happens when a man is forced to become a beast.

As the limo comes to a slow stop in front of the

castle bathed in the dark night, my thumb runs along my hard jaw line, skimming over the deep scar that made me who I am. The glittering candlelight and floral scent that filters in through the cracked tinted windows doesn't hide the ruthlessness of the men attending tonight.

The elite and upper class, better known as the devils in Armani suits that run this city, don't hold a flame to my brutality. They can hide behind the masquerade of tonight, their flutes of expensive champagne and cloaks of luxury, but we all know who we really are. I don't intend to hide behind a damn thing. Just like they don't hide their unease around me.

One of the few partnerships and personal relationships that hasn't changed since then is with a man named Carter Cross. He took what he wanted when it came to *all matters*. I've decided I'm no better.

Annabelle will leave the ball with me tonight. There's nothing that will change my mind of that.

She's beautiful, and the opposite of the beast I became. More than that, the business deals I can acquire with her father's reputation . . . well, he owes me, and I've decided beautiful Belle is what I want in the place of his debt.

Am I sure I want to do this? I answer Alessio with the grim reality, "I've never been more sure of anything in my life."

It's uncomfortable enough in this lace dress that hugs nearly every curve without feeling so many eyes on me. *'A deep red will compliment your complexion,'* my father's public relations director suggested. *'Go dark and sexy, make a show of it and have fun.'* I still remember how she shrugged like it didn't really matter. If it didn't matter, she wouldn't have stepped in at all.

My heels click on the large black and white marble tiled floor in the entry way. Although I can barely hear that over the pounding of my heart as it wrestles against my rib cage to escape.

The chandeliers drip of wealth in this castle. As if the tables topped with ridiculously large bouquets and hors d'oeuvres served on polished silver at every turn of this massive place didn't give it away. It's a masquerade ball set back in time. This elaborate party is ideal to present the newest member of an elite family who runs in my father's circle. As I catch sight of truffles dusted with gold, I wonder how much they spent on renting this castle . . . or if they own it and all this décor was added simply for the show of it all.

I don't belong here for one very important reason. My family is broke, but no one knows it.

The Constantines have money . . . so much more than we do. Which is why PR informed me that I must be present, I must stand out, even, to ensure that stream of money continues to flow into my father's business ventures.

"Miss?" I attempt and fail to hide my shock at the innocent voice at my left. The man dons a simple black mask that only covers his eyes and down to the tip of his nose. All the waiters are wearing them to match their black tuxes. "Champagne?" he offers, and clearing my throat as politely and ladylike as I can, I graciously accept a glass. I'd love about three of them, but I settle on just the one.

"Beautiful mask," he compliments me before nodding and quickly moving on. I don't even have time to thank him. With his back to me, my gaze wanders, but it's quickly diverted when I meet the gaze of a group of men. With their masks on, I'm not sure who is who, but I'm certain they're aware who I am. My mask doesn't conceal my identity in the least.

By design of course. *I must be seen.* The dark red ribbon of lace is hardly a mask at all.

I'm a seductive red rose from head to toe. The designer whispered it with a delighted smile on her face. I could only offer her the same smile and thank you I offered the waiter knowing how much my father needs this.

The champagne is rather bitter on the first sip.

Keeping my clutch close to my side, I walk easily to a lone table and try to decipher who is who. It's impossible, though, with the masks. The vibration against my hip alerts me to a text from my father.

How is it going?

I'm to be the ambassador of sorts for my father. He's older now, and it's simply better to have my face in front of the crowd. Even if they are all older men. Businessmen supposedly, but I've run the books for my father long enough to know.

I'm to look pretty but not speak . . . with that thought in mind, I graciously sip the alcohol. And then a bit more. I'm certainly going to need it.

I've just arrived. I answer him, then silence the phone, slipping it back into the clutch we can't afford. If he wants me to mingle and drop his name and the investments, I can't be on the phone with him.

"Another glass, Miss?" A second waiter, or perhaps the same, they look so alike, holds out his silver tray.

"Thank you." At least I can offer my gratitude this time around.

"I'm so very sorry for your loss," he adds, before dipping slightly.

My heart does a tumble, and my lungs stay still, just as surprised as I am.

"Thank you," I repeat the words spoken in exchange for a glass of champagne as he walks away. They're the only words I seem to know tonight.

My throat is tight, and the next sentence doesn't come. *I appreciate your condolences.* That's what I should say, and I'm aware, but they're too professional . . . too cold. Even though my father and I knew it was coming . . . well, you can never prepare for something like that. My mother's death wasn't sudden, but it was brutal.

As the waiter leaves, a group of three men walk past me, nodding their greetings and hushing whatever conversation they were having.

"Hello, gentlemen," I offer and tip my champagne to them, memorizing their masks and noting that they're at least friendly enough to approach later. I don't know a number of the men here, although some of them are somewhat familiar.

Time ticks, and the crowd thickens. I stay where I am, gathering my composure and forming a plan. Approach, laugh, be conversational, but when the time is right, mention the investments.

I only get one glance around the room, searching for someone who's off on their own, before seeing a face I certainly recognize.

Without the mask, he stands out more than the others. Ever since the books a few months ago. Six to be exact. When my mother became too ill, I took over the finances for my father. It's something only she'd done before.

And when she passed, my father made a deal he shouldn't have, taking out a loan that he couldn't possibly pay off. My fingers slip around the stem of the champagne glass as I take in the man the debt is owed to. Even if we liquidated everything, there's no way Harrison's debt could be paid.

My father never should have done it. The only blessing is that no one here knows. So here I am, to smile and look pretty, and hopefully, new deals will be made in the coming weeks. Even if they are a few weeks past due.

From the whispers I've heard, I would have thought Calum Harrison would stay in the shadows. I thought he'd wear a mask on the half of his face that's scarred.

There's no attempt at hiding from him in the least. With his sharp dark gray suit, tailored perfectly to fit his large muscular frame, he'd stand out even if he tried to hide.

Everyone keeps their distance from him, or so it

would seem. He stands alone, swirling a glass of whiskey in his hand as his gaze sweeps across the room.

He's taller than I thought, more handsome, too. With stubble gracing his skin, I can barely make out the silver line that runs from his cheek down to his throat. It's not the scar, though, that alerted me to who this man is. It's the very air that seems to bend around him.

He is the epitome of dominance. Dark, sharp eyes and a hard jaw line only add to his powerful presence. In a group of ruthless, cutthroat men, he stands out from all the rest.

He can only be the beast. The debt that's owed is owed to this man. The one man in the room I'm not to approach. A direct order from my father.

Like the air around him though, I feel drawn to him.

Until his eyes meet mine, and he steals my breath. My gasp is silent, but the heels of my shoes aren't as I grab my clutch and flee as quickly as I can.

I cannot speak to him. I cannot approach him. I remember the last warning my father gave me: He is a monster.

I repeat the warning in my head as I slip through the crowd. 'Excuse me' is uttered every few steps as I pass guest after guest and questioning gazes through jeweled masks. I nearly trip on the expensive rug leading to a glittering garden away from the main dining hall. It's quiet in the garden, away from prying eyes and away from that man.

It's only once I'm able to sit that I let out a tortured breath. With the shock and innate instinct to run waning, I question what the hell I've just done.

Running all because a man looked at me. But when he did, when that piercing gaze hit mine, I swear he did more than just look at me.

Thank goodness for the champagne.

A deep breath and a sip. I blame my reaction on my nerves and the importance of tonight, until a darkly masculine voice alerts me that someone is here.

Turning slowly, I face the glass doors I've just come from to find the man I was hoping to avoid standing with that same penetrating gaze pinning me in place.

"You weren't invited here." His statement is simple and cutting. If he looked threatening before, all the way across the hall, he looks so much more so in the dim moonlight of the garden. The shadows dance across his handsome face.

"My father—"

"You are not your father," he cuts me off.

With every ounce of strength I have, I answer calmly, "I am here in his place." My palms heat with anticipation, and it's only then that I realize all the ways I react to him. *It's not fear that makes my body bend to his.*

A smirk ticks Harrison's lips up, charming yet cruel in its intention. As if he knows exactly what I've just realized.

Although my thoughts race, I gather my composure and clear my throat. Swallowing thickly, I inform him, "I'm here on my father's behalf, and I can assure you, your debt will be paid.

Harrison's gaze wanders down my body and then back up to meet my own. He makes no response, no sign at all that he heard me.

My body tenses, and I've never felt more like prey caught in the eyes of a hunter.

When he takes his first step, it's not towards me like I thought it would be. Instead, he moves his attention to a blood-red rose and plucks it. My heart races as I watch him move, stealthily and with purpose. There's no one here but us.

"I know it's past due, but I promise he will have every cent to you before the start of the next quarter," I lie, and even to my own ears it sounds like a lie.

He stares at the rose that he twirls between his deft fingers as he speaks. "Do you know the men here?"

"Know them?" I whisper the question, my brow pinched.

"Do you know what they do?" he clarifies, and my heart races.

"They are executives," I speak clearly, although inside I'm screaming.

"Don't lie to me." His voice isn't harsh, but his tone is threatening.

With a tight swallow, I stay calm in my composure and take a single step closer to him. In the moonlight, his gaze shifts to my shoes, then back up. The shards of auburn and gold in his eyes shine back at me.

I answer again. "They are the men who run every aspect of this city. Drug dealers, murderers, and yes . . . executives. They control the wealth and the elected officials. They control everything."

"Wrong." The single word is rushed from his lips and he mirrors my action, taking one step closer to me. "*I* control everything."

A cold sweat lines my skin, a shiver running down my spine as a gust of wind blows by us both. The smell of roses mixes with his masculine scent, and it's heady, nearly dizzying.

I can only nod, "Yes. I know."

"I could have your father killed."

My heart lurches. "No. Please." I nearly go to him, rushing to him to beg him not to, but he closes the distances between us before I can make that move.

Thump, thump, my heart protests, but my body stays right where it is as he towers over me. Slowly, ever so slowly, his hand reaches for my throat. His fingers wrap themselves against my pulse one at a time. And all I can do is look into his eyes. There's so much that swirls in that dark gaze.

"You lie to me."

"No." The attempt at shaking my head in denial is thwarted by his strong grip tightening. It's only a warning.

"You just told me he could make his payment."

My eyes open slowly, but I don't make an attempt to respond.

"I should kill him and set an example. When men take my money and can't pay it back . . ."

"Please," I beg him again. My clutch falls from my grasp to the stones beneath our feet. My trembling fingers reach up to the fine fabric of his suit. "Isn't there anything you want instead?" I question, and I'm very aware that the offer is leading.

So much so that when his eyes drift down my body, I'm certain he can see the hardened peaks of my breasts. I'm not a whore, and I've never offered myself to a man . . . but the tension between us is thick and undeniable.

"Yes, there is. You can take his place."

"Not to die, I hope," I make an effort for my statement to sound as if it's a joke. But with his hand on my throat and the knowledge of what he could do to me, I can't deny fear lingers under the lust.

Leaning closer to me, Harrison drops his lips to the shell of my ear to whisper, "There are many things a man like me requires. I'm sure you can think of something."

There are only two things that keep me from fucking Annabelle on the leather seats of my car right now.

Alessio, my driver; I'm not sharing her moans of pleasure with him or anyone else.

And the second thing . . . my phone going off in my suit jacket. The vibrations haven't stopped since I escorted Miss Belle out of the party.

I've never been harder in my life, walking behind this beautiful rose with everyone's eyes on us. There isn't a single guest that didn't watch in silence as her heels clicked and my hand rested on her back.

Speculation and rumors have already started. I can only imagine what they've conjured up in their heads.

Not a single one of them has the balls to ask though.

Maurizio is the only soul who's called. Time after time, his calls have been persistent, and I'm certain his voicemails are riddled with concern. Perhaps threats at first. Maybe indignation. There's no doubt in my mind that he'll be begging for an answer and to know she's all right in the last message he leaves tonight.

"Harrison." Belle's soft voice grabs my attention. Without the laced ribbon across her face, she's even more alluring. With soft curves and long brunette locks that sweep across her slender shoulders, every inch of her was made to tempt me. She has classic beauty.

Even the way she says my name, questioningly and submissively . . . the desire to take her raw right here and now may win out. "It's Calum . . ."

She clears her throat politely before asking, "Did you know?" There's a brazen tone to her voice that gets my attention.

"Know what?"

"That my father wouldn't be able to pay you." Her lips stay parted just slightly. Her thighs tighten every single time I look her in the eyes.

I could answer her honestly and admit I knew he was a losing bet. I could lie and hide the truth from her. Instead, I settle on something else. "I knew I wanted you. But I didn't know the foreplay would be this . . . enticing."

Her chest rises, and a deep blush blooms in her cheeks.

My phone rings again, interrupting the moment, and I don't hide my annoyance.

"You're a smart girl," I compliment her as I press the ignore button on my phone, sending her father's call straight to voicemail.

"If I'm smart," she practically whispers, her delicate fingers gripping the edge of the leather. The seat protests as she readjusts, attempting not to squirm under my gaze. Licking her lips, she continues, "Then I should know this . . . trip to discuss terms is more than just a trip to discuss terms?" She says each word carefully, and only once she's finished speaking, making her very true statement sound as if it's a question, does she look me in the eye.

The air is thick between us. She already knows the answer.

There's nothing else I want more, and there's no way for her father, Maurizio, to pay.

A text comes through on my phone just as I decide a simple 'yes' will suffice. It halts my answer.

I stare down at the message from Alessio even though Belle's gaze stays on me:

I'm not certain this is for your best interest.

My answer is immediate:

You said yourself, I'm viewed too harshly, too

much of a beast. No one comes to us out of fear, and if I don't soften, I'll lose everything.

His answer comes just as quickly, and I ignore it as the red light in front of us changes to green.

You think blackmail and extortion is softening?

He can call it whatever he'd like. The men I deal with are weak when it comes to violence. Blood-stained streets is how I acquired a good portion of my wealth. They need to see me in a different light, and a woman like Belle by my side will do just that.

"Calum?" Belle whispers my name again, and I'm reminded of the strain against my zipper. Her red-stained lips are parted, and all I can envision is slipping my cock between them.

"Yes. This is much more than discussing terms. You'd be smart to know that," I finally answer her, and this time when my phone vibrates, I simply turn the damn thing off.

ANNABELLE

My shoulders shake with a shuddering breath as the cold breeze from outside is quelled by the front door closing.

Calum's estate is massive, and I stand in the grand foyer in awe.

Riches and wealth drip from every detail of the structure. Yet, it's nearly empty, and the expansive room, heated by a crackling fireplace, still feels cold.

The thud of the locks behind me are what rip my attention away from the carved wood details of the double winding staircase and massive crystal chande-lier that shines down from three stories up.

His large hand rests on the small of my back, just as it did when we left the party. Far too early and abruptly. I can only imagine what the host and guests think.

With Calum leading me, I walk forward, towards the warmth of the fireplace lined with slabs of dark stone that travel from floor to ceiling. I've never felt so small, surrounded by burgundy crushed-velvet furniture and the smell of polished hardwood.

Everything is clean, in its place, and luxurious.

A subtle change forces a small gasp from me. Calum's hand slips from the small of my back to my hip and then slightly lower. Possessively and making no attempts to hide what he wants.

"Shall we have a seat?" he offers, but his gentlemanly question is laced with sin. His front presses against my back as his hand rests on my shoulder. I'm certain I can feel his length against my backside. Sucking in a sharp breath, I wish I could gather the courage to speak.

I've always been a bit too shy to go for what I want.

But that's what led me here, to the mercy of this man. Listening, obeying.

The thought is what convinces me to turn where I am, still close enough to him that we touch, only this time, it's my front to his. With his head lowered and mine raised, I ask him, lust coating my question, "Here then? On the sofa?"

His eyes flash with primitive need, and for a moment I know I've shocked him. He's quick to regain his position, placing his hands on my hips, gently so.

"For now . . . until I have you on your knees on the floor. Or would you rather we get right to it, Belle?"

"On my knees?" The vision flashes in my mind. The crackling of the fire, my knees and palms burning against the rug as Calum takes me from behind, his blunt nails digging into my hips.

A rough groan travels up his chest, once again making me feel as if he's read my mind. "Yes," he answers, "Let's get the formalities over with, and then I'll have you that way first, your ass in the air as I fuck you on all fours."

I couldn't blush any harder, but with the barest grasp on the last bit of dignity I have, I manage to speak. "Is that the deal? My father's debt for tonight?"

Calum's head tilts, and a threat laces the single word he speaks. "Tonight?"

The raging of my heart heats my body, as if I've said something wrong. Instinctively, I take one step back, and he's far too quick to keep us close, matching my step with his own.

"What do you want with me? If not . . . ."

"Oh, I assure you, Belle, what you're thinking is precisely what I want." The desire in his tone is reflected in his gaze, and the lust that rushes in my blood is the only thing that keeps the fear from taking over.

"Then . . . I don't understand." I honestly don't.

"It's going to take much more than a night to pay off your debt."

CALUM

"How much more?" she questions, the desire subsiding, overtaken by the details. "How long is this . . . Arrangement?"

"I'll decide that." Irritation rolls through me, tensing my body. She's already thinking of limiting her time. "I want everything from you. Including your time. As much of it as I desire."

I could give her everything and anything she wanted, but all she wants is to know when it will be over before it's even begun.

"I need to know."

"You don't need to know anything other than how I want you." My words are harsh, and I'm quite aware. She was eager and ready, but panic has reached her eyes.

For the first time since I met her eyes and stalked

her steps at that party, regret lingers in the air between us. My anger quickly dissipates, and the hint of fear bleeds into my thoughts. I almost have her. Ever since I saw her years ago, I've wanted her. I can't let a minor detail take her away from me.

"Did you think one night would pay it all off? That in one night I'd have my fill?" Slipping my hand around the back of her neck, I nip her bottom lip in admonishment, ramping up the desire I know she has for me.

"Calum." Her throat tightens as she swallows. "Please, I need—"

"You need to do as I say," I command her, and my tone resonates, but still she hesitates. I fucking loathe it.

"I will," quickly spoken, her eyes wide and her body willing. "I promise I will. But I need . . ."

"Make it very clear and be quick, Annabelle. My patience is running thin."

"You want to use me, fuck me, and I swear I want you too. How can I agree to letting you do as you please with no way out and no way to stop this . . ."

"When I'm done with you tonight, that won't be a worry. Now, get on your knees."

She gasps, the sound both alarming and tantalizing.

The image embeds itself in my memory.

"You can only have me at night."

"No."

"You expect me here for how long?"

"When I'm here; you're here." My voice is firm. "This isn't negotiable. You'll be taken care of and you'll be ready for me whenever I need."

"And my life?"

"It is owed to me."

"For . . . for however long you decide?"

I can see the likelihood of the next series of events. The fear, her wanting out. She'll make it difficult. More difficult than it needs to be.

"I would prefer not to give you a date. I'd rather give you a word. If you feel the need to be alone. To be without me for a moment. You will come back, and you will continue to be mine in all ways. But if it becomes too intense . . ." My pulse races as she slowly unravels under my offer. The way her eyes turn darker and peer into mine and her lips part just slightly inform me that she's willing, that the offer tempts her.

"Give me a word. Or a statement. Tell me what you'll say if you need . . . a moment. I'm only willing to give you a moment."

"I say this word and you'll let me go?"

"For a day. I'll give you one day and then you must come back."

"A word . . ."

"Or a phrase."

"Deep red rose."

"Deep red rose," I repeat.

"So the terms are: I'm yours to do with as you please. But if it's too much, I have one day if I tell you 'deep red rose'."

Nodding, I hold her gaze, refusing to let it go as she stands in front of me, taking it all in. Did she really think I'd only want her for a night?

"I've grown tired of terms, Belle."

With a sudden inhale, she nods slightly and the tips of her fingers play at the hem of her dress. "How would you like me?" she questions, and I swear I couldn't get harder if I wanted to.

"Good girl," I commend her and take a chance, stalking around her in a slow circle to her back. When I rest my hand at her neck, brushing her hair out of the way, she shivers, and her head falls back slightly. Her quickened breath and the sound of her dress unzipping is all that fills the room. The heat from behind us swells until her dress falls to the floor, followed by her undergarments, and I leave her standing there, bared to me as I unbutton my shirt behind her.

She steals a glance over her shoulder, and I allow it. Taking my time as she stands nervously waiting.

When I unzip my pants, she shifts her weight, her thighs clenching and the blush turning darker against her skin.

With puddles of cloth beside us, I circle her again, gripping and stroking my length. Precum beads on my head and I spread it, stoking myself again.

If I wasn't already an arrogant man, the sight of her eyes widening and her lips parting with a gasp when she stares down at my cock would certainly turn me into one.

With my other hand, I test the weight of her breasts, holding them for a moment and running my thumb against her hardened nipples. Her soft whimper begs for me, and she leans in slightly until I tsk at her.

She's quick to correct herself, even if need is etched into every aspect of her expression.

Her reactions and obedience are perfection. I didn't make a mistake. I was right that she was the perfect one for this.

"Down on your knees and lick," I command her, and she's quick to do just that. I grip myself at the base as she leans forward, gliding her tongue along the veins of my cock. A shudder runs through me as her scandalous tongue slips between my slit, gathering the precum.

My toes curl against the carpet, and my pulse quickens with need. Just as she parts her lips to suck, not lick, I scold her and command her to get on her hands and knees.

The curve of her ass is only outmatched by the

glistening folds that await me. She's ready for me. I don't need to run my fingers along her pussy to know it. But I do. Just to feel her arousal. That small insignificant touch, my fingers drifting from her center to her clit, elicits the sweetest sounds from her. Her eyes close, and she bites down on her lip until I scold her once again.

"I want to hear what I do to you." My wish is spoken as I slip my middle finger inside of her warmth, feeling how tight she is. A strangled gasp fills the air, and I swear I can't take anymore. She's sensitive to every touch.

I could take her slowly, but I have needs, and she should know I'm not a gentle lover. I won't do her the disservice of pretending that I am.

I steady her with one hand gripping her hip, and her body tenses. In a swift stroke I fill her, burying myself to the hilt. Her gorgeous body bows, and she cries out the sweetest sound of pain mixed with pleasure. Staying deep inside of her, I wait for her to adjust, and I'm barely able to contain myself. Leaning down, I rest my chest to her back and kiss just below her ear. With a deep inhale, she peers back at me, looking up through her thick lashes.

Her lips stay parted and her eyes are on mine as I pull out ever so slowly, watching how her eyes dilate and the dangerous cocktail of sinful pleasure rolls through her.

Another thrust, and her head falls forward. With both hands on her hips, I take her brutally and roughly, just as I promised. I groan in time with the sound of our flesh meeting, and Belle cries out her pleasure. It's not long before she tightens around me, nearly making me come before I'm ready as she finds her release.

I allow her another, holding my breath and fucking her until she can no longer stay on all fours. With her front on the carpet, I piston my hips, loving how she writhes under me. I forcefully take her again and again until she cries out my name as if it's a plea. Only then can I finally find my release.

Still recovering and breathing heavily, I lay gentle kisses along the center of her back, running the length of it up to her shoulder. Once I've met the crook of her neck, I slip out of her, and she winces.

Using my shirt, I clean what I can between her thighs. All the while I kiss her, and she turns, facing me and exploring with her own small touches. Her fingers travel up my chest, her nails slipping gently along the grooves of muscle.

"Calum," she moans my name, maybe still lost in the pleasure. I love the sound of my name slipping from her lips. My kiss meets hers, and if only I was still hard, I'd take her again, right here in front of the fire.

In an effort to run her lips along my jaw, she

parts those sweet lips, but I back away. Even with the dim light and the stubble, she'll feel the indentation, her soft kisses will travel along the scar. It's a sharp knife of betrayal that pushes me away from her touch.

"Deep red rose?" she says the phrase I loathe, her escape, but before I can fully absorb it, she corrects herself. "Is that your limit? That's what I meant. You don't want me to touch your scar?"

"No. I don't see why you'd want to."

"Can I?" she questions, her voice full of exhaustion. Ignoring her question, I lift her limp body to the sofa and lay her down.

"Let me get you a blanket . . . or rather. . ." Not finishing the thought, and not bothering to dress myself, I leave her where she is. Replaying the last moment obsessively.

She doesn't flinch, doesn't seem to have any fear at all when it comes to the scar. She doesn't cower at the man I am. Her gentle touch is at odds with everything else. After dressing, I grab the box and return to the living room to find her spread out under the simple throw from the back of the sofa, her hair in a halo, her curves hidden under the luxurious fabric, but still very much on display.

"Can I touch you now?" Her sultry voice carries through the room.

"No."

"Is holding me after out of the question?" she asks, not hiding the longing in her voice.

"Needy girl," I comment, sitting on the end of the sofa where her head rests. The furniture protests with a groan as I take my seat, then I lift her head and set it down onto my lap.

A moment passes of quiet, the glow of the fire our company, and the only conversation the crackling and snapping of the wood.

"How long have you lived like this?" She whispers her question as I pet her hair. How many nights have I sat here alone, lost in work and thoughts of vengeance?

"Like what?" I ask to clarify.

"Alone in such a large place."

"It doesn't matter."

With a saddened tone, she responds, "Small talk never does."

Disliking the way her eyes close and the very idea that she's done with the small talk itself, I answer, "All my life."

It's quiet again, and all I can think as I steal glances at her, with her eyes closed and her dark red lips resting nearly against my leg, is that she's going to say 'deep red rose' any minute. I need to be careful with her, or she'll run.

"You want me to stay here." It's a statement, not a

question. She's already thinking about it. I never should have offered that clause.

"Yes.

"And you won't tell me how long?"

". . . No. But I gave you my word. Your one condition I'll allow." My voice is hard, in stark contrast to hers.

"That's dangerous."

"You'll stay here. You'll do as I like. And the debt will be forgiven."

The fire snaps and hisses with my treatment of her.

Turning slightly on her side, she toys with the blanket between her fingers. Her bare breast peeking from just under the throw.

Lowering my lips to hers, I whisper, "I already want you again."

That gets her attention, and a bit of shock too if her wide eyes peering up at me is anything to go on. They're a beautiful hazel, not unlike the amber fire before us.

"I like that you want me, Mr. Harrison." She hesitates . . . and I wait for it with bated breath. Her escape clause to be uttered from between those gorgeous lips I've yet to use to the fullest.

"I think I like it a little too much. I think you're going to ruin me."

Let me ruin you. The command goes unspoken,

and it's only when she rests her head again that I look up at the clock on the mantel, an ancient thing, but the tick of it is barely audible, and so it stays.

"You have a phone call to make."

"My father?" The cadence of her answer is dreadful.

"Yes, but before that . . . I got you a gift." She's forced to sit up as I pluck the box from the coffee table. This moment is a disturbance, but so long as this is taken care of, I'll have more of her and more of this tonight.

The box leaves my hand and rests in her lap as she sits cross-legged next to me, the throw pooling around, falling slowly, until it's nothing but a puddle of chenille.

It's been a week since I purchased the fine garment and had it delivered. She holds the matte-black box adorned with a satin ribbon.

Instead of opening it, she only runs her fingers along the silk. "You just met me tonight." She tilts her head, questioningly and accusatorily. It stirs something inside of me. Her obedience mixed with curiosity is alluring. I want more of it.

"I knew you'd be there. I knew you'd come home with me."

"You said you knew I wasn't invited."

"I say a lot of things to get what I want." My answer seems to satisfy her.

She unties the ribbon and lifts the silk.

"A silk robe? Rather presumptuous." She doesn't look me in the eyes until the final statement, her slender fingers still running along the fine silk.

"I prefer the term 'confident'. It was only a matter of time, Belle."

"You went through all of this . . . for me?"

"I said I wanted you."

"Why me?"

"Because I saw you, and I imagined something different than what I had for the first time in years. Now put your robe on, it's time to call your father."

It was years ago. For years I've wanted her. If she thinks she can create an end date for this arrangement, she's so very wrong.

"Tell him you're staying here indefinitely."

There's a fine line of pleasure and fear mixed with sadness. Not for me, but for Calum.

We walk the ornate hallway of his home. He could stride past me without any effort. The man is so tall.

His wealth is so vast, this place could be littered with help, yet it's vacant and quiet as far as I can tell.

Calum Harrison could have fucked me in a hall closet of that castle, and I would have loved every second without a single regret.

He could have offered me this deal regardless of my father, and I imagine I would have taken it. Especially now, knowing the divine pleasure that's left me deliciously sore.

The thick wallpaper of deep red paisley lines the hall from floor to ceiling, and although I know this call is going to prove exactly where I stand, I wonder how Calum could even question it.

"You didn't have to do this, you know." I whisper the confrontation. His steady strides that he kept to walk beside me halt, leaving me a hair in front of him. I turn where I am, the fine silk of the evening robe grazing along my skin. Wearing nothing else, it'd be rather scandalous if there were maids or butlers hiding behind the corners.

The little touches he's been giving me make me very aware that Calum enjoys seeing me like this. Wrapped in fine cloth that barely hides a thing from him.

I enjoy it too. In fact . . . I love it.

"It has to happen. You'll call him, inform him that you're with me."

"I don't mean that." I'm aware I interrupt him, but he misunderstood. "Of course I have to call my father."

Content with my response, Calum places his hand on my back, a gesture that we're to continue.

"I would trade anything for my father's life . . . but you could have had my body regardless."

"Your body?"

"You certainly paid a steep price for it."

"Is that right?" he questions, peering down at me. My heart flutters when he looks at me like that. With genuine curiosity. "You think it's only your body I want?"

"No." My answer doesn't come out half as strong with his darkly spoken question. There isn't a doubt in my mind what Calum craves. My submission, my pleasure belonging to him. I have to clear my throat as the dirty thoughts of what he's going to do to me for however long he wants runs a shiver of want down my shoulders.

"You realize this is madness and unnecessary."

"I wanted you and I would do *anything*," he stresses the word, "to really have you."

"But like this?" I can't help but to push.

"I do what I have to do." His hard response doesn't add to the image of the man everyone else sees. All I see in his gaze is desperation.

My heart breaks for him. Truly.

I wonder if he would have gone about it this way before the accident, back when no one referred to him as a beast. Back to articles with him laughing. Back then . . . would he have sought out my father and offered him that deal at his lowest just so he could maneuver a way to keep me in his grasp?

"Do you pity me?" Calum questions, turning towards me and taking a dangerous step closer. The air around him forces me to take a step back, pressing myself against the fine walls of the hallway.

"Pity? No," I answer. He's an enigma, one that my

mind wants to dance with. His hand cups my jaw, holding me captive as the back of my head presses against the wall. "Do you know it turns me on?" I question him back in a whisper. His strength, the force of his entirety. "I've never felt more alive." I only hope he feels the same.

"I could break you."

"I know," I whisper in response to his threatening tone.

"I could do whatever I want to do to you." His lips are closer now and the desire rises up from the pit of my belly.

It only turns me on. *Maybe there's something wrong with me.*

"I saw you years ago," I finally confess to him. "And I made a wish that night; that you would do exactly that." Whatever he wanted.

Calum takes his time slipping the robe from my shoulders. This time when he takes me roughly against the wall, he lets me kiss his scar afterwards.

"I don't care what you tell him; I'm sure he'll have figured it out anyway."

The sound of the first ring is ominous. It seems to slow as my heart races frantically.

Tell him the truth or tell the lie Calum wants to hear. As the phone rings once more, I make the decision simple. Which is the choice I won't regret? Because of the three of us, I'm the only one that will have to live with this decision forever.

"Harrison," my father hisses, and my heart hammers. "If you touched her, I'll destroy you and every—"

"Father," I interrupt him, feeling the ball in my throat grow spikes as I do.

"Annabelle." Relief is evident, but so is fear. "Where are you?"

"Father, please." I swallow and close my eyes at the sound of the hardwood floors creaking behind me as Calum shifts his weight.

Although my father protests, telling me to answer him and questioning where I am again, Calum's hand wraps around my front, splaying across my belly, and he pulls my back into his broad chest.

"I need you to listen to me." My voice is softer, easier with his touch.

All I'm given in response is a curse of frustration. Until he screams, "I'll fucking kill him for hurting you!"

"He didn't hurt me," I object. "I left with him last night because I wanted to." Calum plants a soft kiss below my ear in that sensitive spot that elicits the sweetest of chills down my shoulder.

There is only silence on the other end of the line.

"I'm going to stay with him for a while. I want a break, and I can still—" Just as I'm offering to still do the book-keeping, my father's voice turns questioning.

"If I didn't know any better, I'd think you have feelings for that beast of a man . . ."

"It's something like that . . ."

"This isn't going to end well for you." His voice is foreboding.

It's a tale as old as time, isn't it? Instead of speaking, I offer him silence as Calum breaks away from me, only watching from behind.

"You're making a mistake." My father's tone is harsh.

"I'm making a choice. I want more than this life." I don't know exactly what lies ahead, but it's something more. It's something I never knew how badly I wanted.

"This life?" my father questions with distaste, and then ignores me and what I've just said. They all do. They always have, and I'm tired of being ignored. "Did he threaten you?"

"No."

"Does this have to do with the debt?"

"No." *Lie. Lie after lie.* But I want the beast. I want to live in his dark castle and let him do whatever he wants to me.

"I'm with Calum now. I only called to tell you. I love you."

"Belle, please." Stress lingers over the line from my father's plea. It doesn't matter what he says though, I want this. I want to be captive to Calum. I want him to leave me deliciously used. It's not quite a fairytale, but it's certainly my fantasy.

"I'll call again soon." The old phone clicks as I set it down on Calum's desk, staring at the antique wood and wondering what I've just done. What fate I've chosen.

"Does he believe you?" Harrison's darkly murmured question catches me off guard. I swear this place holds a spell over me. With both of my hands gripping the desk behind me, I face him, the beast I've chosen.

"Does he believe what?" *What were my lies? I* can't even remember. The chill that runs down my spine when Calum peers down at me with his sharp hazel gaze is warmed by the simple touch. At first, it's only the rough pad of his thumb trailing down my jaw. Then it's his hand on my throat, wrapped around it, but not too tight as he plants a single kiss against my lips. The warmth flows just as the desire does, lower and lower to the pit of my belly. When my eyes close, his masculine scent wraps around me, and I can barely breathe.

"It doesn't matter, Belle," he whispers against my lips, and his warm breath travels down the crook of my neck as he plants a kiss there.

The unbuckling of his belt forces my eyes open only to be staring straight ahead at the faint scar along his jaw. Goosebumps travel down my heated skin as he plants one more kiss at the sensitive bit of my neck, just below my ear. My whimper of need is accompanied by his hard chest brushing against my breasts. He whispers, his lips at the shell of my ear, "Get on your knees."

Looking for a darker romance? Merciless is the book for you. Inspired by Beauty and the Beast it's a modern crime family retelling. Read it for free today!

AFTERWORD

I hope you enjoyed reading this collection of short stories!

Looking for more quick, steamy reads? Check out:

Tell Me To Stay (A Novella)
He devoured her, and she did the same to him.
Until it all fell apart and Sophie ran as far away from **Madox** as she could.
After all, the two of them were never meant to be together?

Second Chance (A Novella)
No one knows what happened the night that forced them apart. No one can ever know.
But the moment **Nathan** locks his light blue eyes on

Harlow again, she is ruined.
She never stood a chance.

Burned Promises (A Novella)
Derek made her a promise. And then he broke it.
That's what happens with your first love.
But Emma didn't expect for Derek to fall back into
her life and for her to fall back into his bed.

Want a signed copy of You Have a Piece of My Heart
or any of my other books? Shop here and use
ebook20 to save 20%. Coupon also works on
bookish merch in my shop. Happy shopping xoxo

Click here to sign up to my mailing list, where you'll
get *exclusive* giveaways, free books and new release
alerts!

Follow me on BookBub to be the first to know about
my sales!

Text Alerts:
US residents: Text WILLOW to (302) 205-3701
UK residents: Text WWINTERS to 82228

And if you're on Facebook, join my reader group,
Willow Winters' Wildflowers for special updates and
lots of fun!

ALSO BY WILLOW WINTERS

Small Town Romance

Tequila Rose Book 1
Autumn Night Whiskey Book 2
He tasted like tequila and the fake name I gave him
was Rose.
Four years ago, I decided to get over one man, by
getting under another. A single night and nothing
more.
Now, with a three-year-old in tow, the man I still
dream about is staring at me from across the street in
the town I grew up in. I don't miss the flash of
recognition, or the heat in his gaze.
The chemistry is still there, even after all these years.
I just hope the secrets and regrets don't destroy our
second chance before it's even begun.

A Little Bit Dirty

Contemporary Romance Standalones

Knocking Boots (A Novel)

They were never meant to be together.
Charlie is a bartender with noncommittal tendencies.
Grace is looking for the opposite. Commitment.
Marriage. A baby.

Promise Me (A Novel)
She gave him her heart. Back when she thought
they'd always be together.
Now **Hunter** is home and he wants Violet back.

Tell Me To Stay (A Novella)
He devoured her, and she did the same to him.
Until it all fell apart and Sophie ran as far away from
Madox as she could.
After all, the two of them were never meant to be
together?

Second Chance (A Novella)
No one knows what happened the night that forced
them apart. No one can ever know.
But the moment **Nathan** locks his light blue eyes on
Harlow again, she is ruined.

She never stood a chance.

Burned Promises (A Novella)
Derek made her a promise. And then he broke it.
That's what happens with your first love.
But Emma didn't expect for Derek to fall back into
her life and for her to fall back into his bed.

You Are Mine World

You Are My Reason (You Are Mine Duet book 1)
You Are My Hope (You Are Mine Duet book 2)
Mason and Jules emotionally gripping romantic
suspense duet.
One look and Jules was tempted; one taste, addicted.
No one is perfect, but that's how it felt to be in
Mason's arms.
But will the sins of his past tear them apart?

You Know I Love You
You Know I Need You
Kat says goodbye to the one man she ever loved even
though **Evan** begs her to trust him.
With secrets she couldn't have possibly imagined, Kat
is torn between what's right and what was right for
them.

Tell Me You Want Me

A sexy office romance with a brooding hero, **Adrian Bradford**, who you can't help but fall head over heels for... in and out of the boardroom.

Valetti Crime Family Series:
A HOT mafia series to sink your teeth into.

Dirty Dom
Becca came to pay off a debt, but **Dominic Valetti** wanted more.
So he did what he's always done, and took what he wanted.

His Hostage
Elle finds herself in the wrong place at the wrong time. The mafia doesn't let witnesses simply walk away.
Regret has a name, and it's **Vincent Valetti**.

Rough Touch
Ava is looking for revenge at any cost so long as she can remember the girl she used to be.
But she doesn't expect **Kane** to show up and show her kindness that will break her.

Cuffed Kiss
Tommy Valetti is a thug, a mistake, and everything

Tonya needs; the answers to numb the pain of her past.

Bad Boy
Anthony is the hitman for the Valetti familia, and damn good at what he does. They want men to talk, he makes them talk. They want men gone, bang - it's done. It's as simple as that.
Until Catherine.

Those Boys Are Trouble (Valetti Crime Family Collection)

To Be Claimed Saga
A hot tempting series of fated love, lust-filled secrets and the beginnings of an epic war.

Wounded Kiss
Gentle Scars

Read Willow's sexiest and most talked about romances in the Merciless World

This Love Hurts Trilogy
This Love Hurts
But I Need You
And I Love You the Most

An epic tale of both betrayal and all-consuming love...
Marcus, the villain.
Cody Walsh, the FBI agent who knows too much.
And Delilah, the lawyer caught in between.

What I Would do for You (This Love Hurts Trilogy Collection)

A Kiss to Tell (a standalone novel)
They lived on the same street and went to the same school, although he was a year ahead. Even so close, he was untouchable.
Sebastian was bad news and Chloe was the sad girl who didn't belong.
Then one night changed everything.

Possessive (a standalone novel)
It was never love with **Daniel Cross** and she never thought it would be. It was only lust from a distance. Unrequited love maybe.
He's a man Addison could never have, for so many reasons.

Merciless Saga
Merciless
Heartless
Breathless

Endless

Ruthless, crime family leader **Carter Cross** should've known Aria would ruin him the moment he saw her. Given to Carter to start a war; he was too eager to accept. But what he didn't know was what Aria would do to him. He didn't know that she would change everything.

All He'll Ever Be (Merciless Series Collection of all 4 novels)

Irresistible Attraction Trilogy
A Single Glance
A Single Kiss
A Single Touch

Bethany is looking for answers and to find them she needs one of the brothers of an infamous crime family, **Jase Cross**.
Even a sizzling love affair won't stop her from getting what she needs.
But Bethany soon comes to realise Jase will be her downfall, and she's determined to be his just the same.

Irresistible Attraction (A Single Glance Trilogy Collection)

Hard to Love Series
Hard to Love
Desperate to Touch
Tempted to Kiss
Easy to Fall

Eight years ago she ran from him.
Laura should have known he'd come for her. Men like
Seth King always get what they want.
Laura knows what Seth wants from her, and she
knows it comes with a steep price.
However it's a risk both of them will take.

Not My Heart to Break (Hard to Love Series
Collection)

Tease Me Once
Tease me once... I'll kiss you twice.
Declan Cross' story from the Merciless World.

Spin off of the Merciless World

Love the Way Series
Kiss Me
Hold Me
Love Me

With everything I've been through, and the

unfortunate way we met, the last thing I thought I'd be focused on is the fact that I love the way you kiss me.

Extended epilogues to the Merciless World Novels
A Kiss To Keep (more of Sebastian and Chloe)
Seductive (more of Daniel and Addison)
Effortless (more of Carter and Aria)
Never to End (more of Seth and Laura)

Sexy, thrilling with a touch of dark Standalone Novels

Broken (Standalone)
Kade is ruthless and cold hearted in the criminal world.
They gave Olivia to him. To break. To do as he'd like. All because she was in the wrong place at the wrong time. But there are secrets that change everything. And once he has her, he's never letting her go.

Forget Me Not (Standalone novel)
She loved a boy a long time ago. He helped her escape and she left him behind. Regret followed her every day after.
Jay, the boy she used to know, came back, a man. With a grip strong enough to keep her close and a look in his eyes that warned her to never dare leave him again.

It's dark and twisted.
But that doesn't make it any less of what it is.
A love story. Our love story.

It's Our Secret (Standalone novel)
It was only a little lie. That's how stories like these
get started.
But with every lie Allison tells, **Dean** sees through it.
She didn't know what would happen. But with all the
secrets and lies, she never thought she'd fall for him.

Collections of shorts and novellas

Don't Let Go
A collection of stories including:
Infatuation
Desires in the Night and Keeping Secrets
Bad Boy Next Door

Kisses and Wishes
A collection of holiday stories including:
One Holiday Wish
Collared for Christmas
Stolen Mistletoe Kisses

All I Want is a Kiss (A Holiday short)
Olivia thought fleeting weekends would be enough

and it always was, until the distance threatened to tear her and **Nicholas** apart for good.

Highest Bidder Series:

Bought
Sold
Owned
Given
From USA Today best selling authors, Willow Winters and Lauren Landish, comes a sexy and forbidden series of standalone romances.

Highest Bidder Collection (All four Highest Bidder Novels)

Bad Boy Standalones, cowritten with Lauren Landish:

Inked
Tempted
Mr. CEO
Three novels featuring sexy powerful heroes. Three romances that are just as swoon-worthy as they are tempting.

Simply Irresistible (A Bad Boy Collection)

Forsaken, (A Dark Romance cowritten with B. B. Hamel)
Grace is stolen and gifted to him; Geo a dominating, brutal and a cold hearted killer.
However, with each gentle touch and act of kindness that lures her closer to him, Grace is finding it impossible to remember why she should fight him.

View Willow's entire collection and full reading order at willowwinterswrites.com/reading-order

Happy reading and best wishes,
Willow xx

ABOUT WILLOW WINTERS

Thank you so much for reading my romances. I'm
just a stay at home mom and avid reader turned
author and I couldn't be happier.
I hope you love my books as much as I do!

More by W Winters
www.willowwinterswrites.com/books/

Sign up for my Newsletter to get all my romance
releases, sales, sneak peeks and a **FREE** Romance,
Burned Promises

If you prefer *text alerts* so you don't miss any of my
new releases, text
US residents: Text WILLOW to 797979

UK residents: Text WWINTERS to 82228

CONTACT W WINTERS
BOOKBUB | TWITTER | GOODREADS | TIKTOK
INSTAGRAM | FACEBOOK PAGE | WEBSITE

Check out Willow Winters Wildflowers on Facebook
- If I'm not writing, I'm there!

www.ingramcontent.com/pod-product-compliance
Lightning Source LLC
Chambersburg PA
CBHW031045310726

48969CB00007B/2130